replica

Dreamcrusher

MARILYN KAYE

BANTAM BOOKS
NEW YORK • TORONTO • LONDON • SYDNEY • AUCKLAND

RL 5.5, 008–012

DREAMCRUSHER

A Bantam Skylark Book / August 2001

ISBN 0-553-48747-7

Visit us on the Web! www.randomhouse.com/kids

Published simultaneously in the United States and Canada

Bantam Skylark is an imprint of Random House Children's Books, a division of
Random House, Inc. SKYLARK BOOK and colophon and BANTAM BOOKS
and colophon are registered trademarks of Random House, Inc. Bantam Books,
1540 Broadway, New York, New York 10036.

PRINTED IN THE UNITED STATES OF AMERICA

OPM   10   9   8   7   6   5   4   3   2   1

For Marianne Mowry Gardner

Dreamcrusher

one

There wasn't a cloud in the sky that Saturday afternoon. The sun shone so brightly on the beach that there appeared to be diamonds hidden among the grains of sand. The water was warm, and white-crested waves were just the right size for bodysurfing. A hint of a breeze was just enough to keep the air from being too sultry.

Lying on a beach towel, Amy Candler was thinking it was a perfect day for a birthday beach party. And she knew that the birthday girl, Jan Rosen, had to be very happy about this. Jan sat next to Amy in math class,

and all week long she'd been worrying about the possibility of a Saturday shower. Amy had constantly assured her that the weather would be fine. Of course,
Amy had no way of knowing that for sure, and she certainly couldn't guarantee a pretty day, but she knew
this was what Jan wanted to hear. In any case, Jan had
lucked out, and so had the dozen kids she'd invited to
her party.

In a huge, brightly striped tent set up on the beach,
they'd all stuffed themselves on barbecued chicken,
macaroni salad, and birthday cake. Now three kids
were tossing Frisbees in the water while others were
playing beach volleyball. Amy was perfectly content to
lie in the sun and soak up the rays. Her best friend,
Tasha Morgan, plopped down next to her and let out
an exaggerated sigh.

"Look at Simone Cusack," she directed Amy.

Amy obliged, opening one eye and looking. "What
about her?"

"Can you believe what she's wearing? That bikini,
it's so, so . . . not there."

"It is pretty skimpy," Amy agreed. "But she looks
nice." She closed her eye.

"I know," Tasha said mournfully. "I wish I could
wear a swimsuit like that."

"You could have a bikini if you wanted one," Amy said.

"No way, I'm too fat. Why did you let me eat two pieces of cake?"

"Because I'm not the food police," Amy replied patiently. They'd had conversations like this before, and Amy always said pretty much the same thing. "And just because you're not as skinny as Simone doesn't mean you're fat. Besides, you're prettier than Simone."

"Peter doesn't think so," Tasha said.

Reluctantly, Amy opened both her eyes and focused on Peter Weston. True, he was staring at Simone. But then, so were most of the boys. Amy was sure that Simone had worn the bikini to get just that kind of attention.

But Tasha had referred only to Peter, and that set off an alarm in Amy's head. "Do you have a crush on Peter Weston?"

"It's not a crush," Tasha replied indignantly. "I just, kind of, you know, sort of like him. Do you think he's cute?"

"He's okay," Amy acknowledged.

"He waited for me after math yesterday," Tasha said dreamily. "He's into basketball, and he heard that my brother is the only tenth grader on the high school varsity team. But I think he was just using that as an excuse to talk to me."

"Maybe," Amy allowed. "Did you talk about anything else?"

"Oh, sure, we talked about this party, and what we were giving Jan for her birthday. And we talked about homework. You're so lucky not to be in our class, Amy. Mr. Henderson is evil." The ringing of a bell down the beach caught her attention. "Hey, there's the ice cream truck. You want an ice cream bar?"

It had been at least an hour since the cake, and Amy could manage another treat. "Okay. See if they've got caramel crunch. If not, get me a coconut ripple. No, banana fudge. There's some change in my bag."

"You can pay me later. Banana fudge . . ."

"Only if he doesn't have caramel crunch," Amy cautioned her.

"Be right back. Oh, hi, Chris. You want something from the ice cream truck?"

"No thanks."

Amy smiled at Chris Skinner and edged over to make room for him on her towel. "How was the water?"

"Okay. Not cold." He sat down, but he didn't look at her. He was watching the volleyball players. Probably Simone in particular.

Amy struggled into a sitting position. "You want to play volleyball?" she asked.

"No," Chris said. "Do you?"

"Not really. It's so nice just lying in the sun." She didn't add that playing any sport was always a risk for her. There was always the chance she'd play too well. In the spirit of competition, she might forget herself and reveal just how exceptional her physical capabilities were.

Chris had stopped watching the volleyball players and was now looking at Amy. Actually, he seemed to be staring at her back. "You have a tattoo!" he remarked in surprise.

"No, I don't."

"The crescent moon on your right shoulder—it's not a tattoo?"

"No, it's a birthmark."

"Huh. I never saw a birthmark like that."

That statement didn't require a response, and Amy didn't offer one. She couldn't tell Chris what the crescent moon was all about, not yet. If he stuck around and they remained boyfriend and girlfriend, and she felt she could trust him completely, maybe someday she'd reveal all.

Lately, though, she'd been doubting that *someday*

would ever come. Chris had been acting strange, sort of distant, as if something was bothering him.

She recalled what Tasha had said about math. Chris was in that class too. "Is Mr. Henderson getting you down?"

"Huh?"

"Tasha says he's a beast."

"Oh. Yeah, he's strict, I guess. But he's not a bad teacher. At least I can figure out what he's talking about."

So it wasn't school. Probably something more personal. That wouldn't be too surprising. Chris had a very unusual personal life.

Tasha returned with three ice cream bars. "They didn't have caramel crunch," she told Amy. "And I couldn't remember if you wanted banana fudge or coconut ripple, so I got you both."

"I'll take the banana fudge," Amy said. "Chris, you want the coconut ripple?"

"No, I'm not hungry."

That was a lie, and Amy knew it. Chris was always hungry. "It's going to melt if you don't eat it. It shouldn't go to waste."

"And I didn't have to pay for it," Tasha added. "It was a special deal-of-the-day or something. Three for the price of two."

Amy shot her friend a look of warm appreciation. It was a good story. Tasha knew as well as Amy did that Chris couldn't buy ice creams the way the rest of them could. Abandoned by crummy parents, he slept in a homeless shelter, and he only had money when he could pick up odd jobs in the neighborhood.

"Well, if it's just going to waste," Chris murmured, and accepted the ice cream.

Tasha tore the wrapper off her own chocolate-mint-chip bar. "So, what's the topic of conversation? Tell me if it's getting romantic and I'll take a walk."

"No, we're talking about math," Amy told her. "Chris says Henderson's an okay teacher."

"Yeah, I guess so," Tasha admitted. "He loves math. He just hates kids."

The volleyball game was breaking up, and some kids were running into the ocean. Two guys were swinging Simone in the air, pretending they were going to toss her into the water. One of the guys was Peter. Simone was shrieking and clearly loving every minute of it.

Tasha watched glumly. "I'm going on a diet," she announced.

Jan, the birthday girl, ran over to join them. "You guys having fun?"

Amy tried to make up for Chris's silence and Tasha's morose expression. "Absolutely—it's a great party."

"Have you done the math assignment yet?" Jan asked her. "Is it hard?"

No math assignment, or any other kind of homework, was ever very hard for Amy, but that was another secret she had to keep to herself. "Not bad. It's only four problems."

"You guys are so lucky you don't have Henderson," Tasha said. "He piles on the homework every weekend."

"I heard he hands out pencils and collects them after class," Jan remarked.

Tasha nodded. "He says it's because he's sick of kids claiming they never have pencils. He's always telling us how irresponsible we are."

"Speaking of irresponsible," Jan said, "don't forget to pick up those ice cream wrappers, okay? My father's a police officer, and it would look really bad if people got littering tickets at his own daughter's party."

Amy gathered up the wrappers and took them to a trash can. When she returned, Chris had disappeared and Tasha was leafing through a magazine. Amy decided it was time to give her back a chance to tan. She lay down on her stomach, rested her head on her hands, and closed her eyes.

When she heard the lifeguard's shrill whistle, she realized she must have fallen asleep. Otherwise, she would have noticed the sudden change in the weather. The temperature must have dropped ten degrees.

She looked at the sky in alarm. Huge, almost black clouds had moved in, blocking the sun. A streak of lightning crossed the sky, followed by a clap of thunder.

The lifeguard blew his whistle again. Everyone was getting out of the water. Drops of rain began to fall, and the kids ran toward the tent. Amy got up and started running in that direction too. There was another streak of lightning, another crash of thunder, and the rain began coming down harder.

More lightning. It seemed to light up the sky. Another streak, even brighter, almost blinding. Amy thought she heard someone screaming. It was strange, because it sounded near and far at the same time. And she felt so strange, so tingly.

Then she felt nothing.

two 2

Was she having that old nightmare again? It had been so long since she'd dreamed of the laboratory. It wasn't exactly the same this time, but it was awfully familiar.

She was lying on her back, helpless but not uncomfortable. Everything around her was white—the walls, the ceiling—and it seemed very clean. She could hear a rhythmic ticking and soft voices. But she wasn't enclosed in glass, the way she was in the old nightmare. So maybe there wouldn't be any fire this time.

The recurring dream used to scare her and wake her up. Now that she understood what it meant, it didn't frighten her anymore. She knew that the dream was a faint recollection, a memory of her birth, or her creation or evolution, or whatever it was called when an artificially conceived, genetically designed clone was taken out of an incubator. Amy had been clone Number Seven of thirteen and the last to be rescued before the laboratory went up in flames.

"Amy! Amy, can you hear me?"

A man's voice . . . Dr. Jaleski's? No, Dr. Jaleski was dead.

"Amy!"

Now the man was snapping his fingers in her face. How rude . . . but then Amy heard another voice, a woman's anxious one.

"Amy, darling, please, answer us!"

Amy blinked away the hazy feeling, and her mother's concerned face became recognizable. Dr. Dave, her mother's friend and former colleague, was there too. She realized that she hadn't been dreaming after all—she was lying on her back, surrounded by white walls, and in the background she heard the soft thump of a heart monitor.

But this wasn't a laboratory—this was a hospital. And Amy was a patient.

She found her voice. "Wha—what happened?"

"You were struck by lightning on the beach," Dr. Dave told her. "It knocked you out."

"But you're going to be okay," Nancy Candler quickly assured her. "Isn't that right, Dave?"

"Absolutely," the doctor said. "I've run a whole battery of tests, X rays, a CAT scan, a cardiogram, the works. They all checked out fine. The EEG showed some increase in brain activity, but that's not unusual after a strong electric shock. Everything's normal." He winked. "Relatively speaking, that is."

Amy managed to wink back, and then she winced. For a brief second, the room had been spinning.

"We're going to let you rest for a while," her mother said. "Then I can take you home."

"Okay," Amy murmured. She didn't mind the idea of a little rest. That slight dizziness was making her uncomfortable, and she wasn't exactly ready to leap off the table.

Her mother kissed her lightly on the forehead; then she and Dr. Dave retreated. Alone, Amy took some deep breaths and tried to pull herself together. She remembered the beach and the sudden storm, but after that everything was a blank. Someone must have called 911 for an ambulance, and Tasha must have told them to take her to this particular hospital, where Dr. Dave ran the emergency room. Of all the kids at the beach party, Tasha was the only one who knew that Amy had to be treated by Dr. Dave and no one else. He knew what Amy was all about.

He had worked with Nancy Candler on Project Crescent more than thirteen years ago. The team of scientists had combined exceptional genes and replicated them to create the female clones. They thought their experiments would benefit humanity by reducing the possibilities of genetic disorders. Instead, they learned that their project had been funded by a mysterious organization intent on creating a superior race of beings. The project had been abandoned and the evidence destroyed—but the clones had been saved and distributed for adoption throughout the world. Nancy Candler had taken Number Seven home to raise as her own daughter.

It had been more than a year since Amy had discovered her heritage. She was aware of the positive and negative aspects of her unique nature. On the positive side, she was superior in every possible way—stronger, healthier, smarter, and more talented than others her age. In fact, both physically and intellectually, she was pretty close to perfect.

But there was one drawback. Her existence had to be kept a secret. Unless she wanted to end up as an object of experimentation, constantly studied and probed, she had to appear as a normal, run-of-the-mill thirteen-year-old girl. It wasn't always easy keeping her special qualities under wraps.

One of the greatest benefits of her superior genes was her ability to recover quickly—bruises, cuts, even broken bones healed rapidly. Now, only moments after she had awakened from unconsciousness, the mild dizziness she had felt was gone. She swung her legs over the side of the table and hopped off.

Her mother returned with some clothes. "How are you feeling?" she asked anxiously.

"Fine," Amy replied. "Can we go now?"

Dr. Dave came back to give her a quick checkup and said they could take off. They left the emergency room and headed down the hall toward the hospital's exit.

Amy wrinkled her nose. She didn't much like the smell of hospitals. And a hospital's sights weren't pleasant at all. There were injuries, people in pain, blood . . . and, of course, a lot of unhappiness. As they passed a waiting area, Amy saw a woman with her face buried in her hands, crying softly. Amy could hear the fear and anxiety in her sobs, and her heart ached.

Impulsively, Amy left her mother's side and touched the woman's arm. "Don't worry, it's okay," she said soothingly.

The woman uncovered her face. "What?"

"Your little boy . . . he'll live. He's going to be just fine."

The woman didn't respond, and now her tear-stained face showed confusion as well as sorrow.

"Amy!" There was a mild rebuke in her mother's tone. Amy returned to her side.

"You shouldn't have said that," Nancy admonished her. "You have no idea what's going on with her little boy. You shouldn't offer assurances when you don't even know what's wrong. You could be giving false hope."

Amy felt her face redden. Her mother was right, of course. She wasn't even sure why she'd spoken to the poor woman. As Nancy strode on toward the door, Amy hesitated. Should she apologize?

That turned out not to be necessary. A doctor came into the waiting area, ripping his white mask off his face and smiling at the woman.

"He's going to be fine," he told her. "The injuries were minor, and there was no internal damage. He's in the recovery room now. You can see him."

Looking enormously relieved and thanking the doctor, the woman followed him. Amy beamed.

"Amy!"

She hurried to catch up with her mother. She was

about to report on the good news she'd overheard when another thought took precedence. "Let's go to Presto Pizza," she suggested.

"What?"

"Don't you want to get something to eat?" Amy asked.

Nancy smiled. "You know, I was just thinking about how hungry I am. And a pizza is exactly what I'm craving."

three

On Monday morning, Amy opened the door to Tasha and anticipated her question. "I'm fine," Amy assured her friend. "No side effects. I don't feel dizzy or anything."

"Great," Tasha said in relief. "How do I look?"

This was not a question Tasha usually asked in the mornings. Amy looked her over and tried to see if anything was new or different. "You look good, just like you always do."

Tasha was disappointed with her response. "Not any thinner? I started my diet yesterday."

"I think it'll take more than a day before anyone can see a difference," Amy told her.

"Yeah, I know," Tasha sighed. "I just thought that with your super-vision, you might see some shrinkage before other people."

"Oh, I'm sure I will," Amy said quickly. "And I'll let you know the minute I do." She made a mental note to remark on Tasha's thinness in a few days, even if she didn't see any change. A person always knew what a best friend wanted to hear. "Mom! I'm going to school!"

"Have a nice day," her mother called back, and Amy stepped outside.

"I hope you're not on one of those crazy crash diets," she said to Tasha. "You don't want to starve yourself."

"It's nothing like that," Tasha assured her. "It's a very sensible and healthy diet, with lots of fruits and vegetables. Medically approved, especially for teens. I found it in a magazine."

That sounded okay to Amy, but now something else was bothering her. She couldn't put her finger on it, but something made her look back at Tasha's door. Eric, Tasha's older brother, was coming out. She must have heard him; that was why she felt a little uneasy.

Eric used to be Amy's boyfriend. And she still considered him a plain old friend—sort of. At least, he wasn't an enemy. But ever since he'd started high school that year, he'd been behaving obnoxiously. He acted like he was way too cool and mature to be hanging out with middle-school students.

His attitude showed even in the way he sauntered over to them with a superior expression on his face. Tasha couldn't bear her brother's new arrogance any more than Amy could. She addressed him sternly.

"Weren't you supposed to be at school fifteen minutes ago?"

Eric responded with a nonchalant shrug. He was carrying a bag of M&M's, and he shoved a handful of candy into his mouth. "NBD," he mumbled.

Amy tried to sound as stern as Tasha. "You shouldn't talk with your mouth full, it's rude. And what does NBD mean?"

Eric swallowed. "No big deal." He shook his head wearily, as if appalled by the fact that they didn't know the latest slangy abbreviations. Like everybody was too busy to say entire words. So dumb, Amy thought.

Eric extended the bag to her. "Want some?"

"No thanks."

"Not for me either," Tasha said. "I'm on a diet."

"Yeah, sure you are." Eric laughed. "How long is that going to last?"

"It's going to last until I'm as thin as Simone Cusack," Tasha replied.

Eric turned to Amy. "Wanna bet on it? I say she'll stick to it two days, tops. What do you think?"

"I have no intention of betting on my best friend," Amy said. "Excuse us, Eric. *We* don't want to get detention." She took Tasha's arm and started off, knowing that Eric had to head in the opposite direction to reach the high school.

"Thanks for sticking up for me," Tasha said. "I shouldn't have told him I was on a diet. Now he'll tease me every chance he gets."

"He'd find out anyway, when you don't take desserts at dinner," Amy said. "But, Tasha, you don't really need to be on a diet, you know. Like I keep telling you, you're not fat. You should have more self-esteem. You're very pretty, and you're smart, and you're an outstanding person just the way you are. You're editor of the *Parkside News,* for crying out loud! That's a very big deal!"

Tasha wasn't convinced. "I'll bet Peter doesn't think it's a big deal. He'd be more interested in me if I looked like Simone."

"Peter doesn't care if you're fat or thin," Amy informed her. "And he's going to ask you for a date even before you've lost any weight."

Tasha sighed. "You're just saying that to make me feel better."

"No, I'm not," Amy said. "I mean it."

"Don't be silly," Tasha retorted. "You hardly know Peter—how can you know what he's going to do?" Then her expression turned hopeful. "Unless he told someone, like Chris, and Chris told you!"

"No, Chris didn't tell me anything," Amy said. Actually, she wasn't sure *why* she'd told Tasha that Peter would ask her out. Probably just to make her feel better, like Tasha said.

When they arrived at school, Amy found herself the center of attention on the front steps. Everyone had heard about what happened to her on the beach, and they had a million questions.

"What did it feel like, getting hit by lightning?"

"Was it like a massive electric shock?"

"Did it hurt?"

"I don't remember," Amy confessed. "One minute I was on the beach, the next minute I woke up in the hospital. My memory's a blank."

"So you just had a little teensy-tiny bit of brain damage, huh?" someone teased.

"I'm going to the *News* office and check the mail before homeroom," Tasha told Amy.

"Okay," Amy said. "See you in math."

Tasha laughed. "No, you won't. We're not in the same math class."

She was right, of course. Amy frowned. "I guess I meant, See you in English. Hey, maybe that lightning *did* affect my brain."

She went on to her own homeroom. It was early, so only a few others were in the room. Amy took her seat beside Linda Riviera, who barely looked at her and muttered "Hi" in a not-too-friendly way.

Amy was used to that kind of greeting from her. Linda was always snotty to her, mainly because of what had happened to Linda's best friend, Jeanine Bryant, who had been Amy's enemy since first grade. Jeanine had been killed when she was pushed down some school stairs, and for a while people like Linda had suspected Amy of pushing her. Eventually they'd found out who the real villain was, but Linda still didn't much like Amy.

But she likes my sweater, Amy thought. She wants one just like it. She'd never tell me that, though.

Then her forehead puckered. How did she know that Linda envied her sweater? Maybe she'd read something in the way Linda looked at her. But Linda hadn't given her more than the briefest possible glance.

Students began to pour in and the bell rang. The homeroom teacher, Ms. Weller, took her place at the front desk and called the roll. Then the intercom came on.

"May I have your attention for the morning announcements?" the hollow voice of the assistant principal echoed. "Seventh-grade students are reminded that permission slips for the field trip are due in the office tomorrow. Tryouts for the chorus will be held at three-thirty today and tomorrow in room 209. Today's Spanish club meeting has been canceled."

She went on with more stuff like that—extracurricular activities, upcoming special events. None of the announcements affected Amy, but something at the end caught her attention.

"Some of you may have heard that Ms. Kanter was injured this weekend in an accident."

Amy's head jerked up. Ms. Kanter was her math teacher.

"I've just spoken to her on the phone," the assistant principal continued. "She broke her leg in several places. She's going to be all right, but she'll be out of school for at least a month."

That was too bad, Amy thought. She liked Ms. Kanter. Maybe Amy should get the other students together and send the teacher a card or flowers.

"Those of you who are in Ms. Kanter's classes have been reassigned temporarily to other classes. If you are in Ms. Kanter's first-period class, you will report to Mr. Mueller's class in room 120. Second period will join Ms. Parks in 101."

Amy listened carefully to hear where her fourth-period math class would go.

"Ms. Kanter's fourth-period class will be combined with Mr. Henderson's class in room 222."

Amy's mouth dropped open. She had said "See you in math" to Tasha—and now she really would be seeing her in math! What a funny coincidence.

fur

Amy watched the clock on the classroom wall as the minute hand inched its way toward twelve. Too bad her powers didn't include the ability to make time move faster. She was hungry. Clearly, being struck by lightning hadn't affected her appetite.

Layne, sitting next to her, was also watching the clock. "I'm *starving*," she said. "I hope it's macaroni and cheese today."

Amy liked the cafeteria's macaroni and cheese too, and wished it were on the menu. "They're serving meat loaf," she told Layne.

"On Monday?" Layne said. "It's usually chicken or

soup and sandwiches or macaroni and cheese on Mondays."

Layne was right. The cafeteria didn't have a strict menu, but there were routines. Meat loaf usually turned up toward the end of the week—students joked that it was the ground-up leftovers of the previous days. Why had Amy said there would be meat loaf today? She shrugged. "Just a guess," she told Layne.

But it was a good guess. Moments later, in the cafeteria line, Layne peered ahead to see what was being offered. "It *is* meat loaf!" she told Amy. "How did you know?"

How *had* she known? "Maybe I saw the trays earlier," she said, "and I just forgot." But she usually had an excellent memory, even for the most insignificant details. She hoped the lightning bolt hadn't affected *that*.

As they waited in line, they talked about math. Layne had the same teacher as Amy, but in a different period. "Who do *you* have for math now?" Layne asked her.

"Henderson," Amy replied.

Layne was immediately sympathetic. "I heard he's a beast."

"Yeah, that's what I heard too," Amy acknowledged. "Everyone says he's smart but he hates kids."

"I don't get it," Layne said. "Why do people who hate kids become teachers?"

"For the money?" Amy wondered aloud.

"No, they don't get paid all that much," Layne said. They were approaching the people who served the food, and she lowered her voice. "And teachers aren't the only ones in school who hate kids."

Amy knew who she was referring to. Most of the people who worked in the cafeteria were pleasant, but one woman never smiled and glared at them like they were going to grab more food than they were entitled to. As if anyone really craved school cafeteria food.

Amy gazed at that particular woman curiously. She really did have a nasty expression on her face. Her eyebrows were so thick they practically met above her nose. Maybe that was why she always looked angry. Or maybe she really was having mean thoughts about the kids. Like, like . . .

Rotten, spoiled kids. If I hear one more complaint about meat loaf, I'll throw it in their ugly faces. Or I'll put rat poison in their food and watch them all keel over in agony and throw up. Or maybe they'll die. Even better.

Amy drew in her breath so sharply that Layne glanced at her oddly. "You okay?"

"Fine," Amy managed to say, but she really wasn't. She looked at the cafeteria woman again. She supposed the woman *could* be having evil thoughts—but how would Amy know?

"Are you going to take this tray or not?" the woman snapped at her. "You're holding up the line!"

"Sorry," Amy murmured. She took the tray. "I like meat loaf," she added impulsively.

Sarcastic little brat.

Had the woman actually said that to her? Amy grabbed the tray and practically ran to her usual table, where Tasha was already waiting for her. Tasha was gazing at her food glumly.

"I should start bringing my lunch from home," she said as Amy sat down. "It seems like such a waste of calories to eat this garbage."

"If you put ketchup on the meat loaf, it's okay," Amy told her.

Tasha reached into her bag and pulled out a small pamphlet.

"What's that?" Amy asked.

"It tells you what foods are fattening." Tasha flipped some pages and groaned. "There's sugar in ketchup, and I'm not supposed to have sugar."

"There couldn't be that much," Amy pointed out.

30

"It's not like ketchup is really sweet. I'm sure it's okay to have a little."

Tasha glared at her. "Hey, are you going to support me or not? Don't tell me to eat things I'm not supposed to have! And you should try to stop me if I'm tempted!"

"Okay, okay," Amy said hastily. "Boy, you're in a crummy mood."

Tasha nodded. "Peter didn't even speak to me when I saw him in the hall last period. And you said he was going to ask me out!"

Amy shifted uncomfortably. She should never have said that. "Well, it's not like I could really know, could I? Hey, isn't it funny that I'm going to be in math with you after I said 'See you in math' this morning?"

"You won't think it's so funny once you've had a dose of Mr. Henderson," Tasha muttered.

"Oh, come on, he can't be *that* bad," Amy said. But thirty minutes later, when she entered Mr. Henderson's classroom, she had to admit she was feeling a little apprehensive.

The room was packed with students, and people were bringing in extra chairs. One of them had been placed by Chris's seat, and Amy grabbed it.

"Hi!" she greeted him.

He returned the greeting, but his smile wasn't as quick as it used to be, and his eyes had that distant look she'd been noticing lately. Yes, something was bothering him, but she didn't think she should ask him what was up. He'd tell her when he was ready to share his problem, whatever it was. Surely it couldn't just be about the sweater she was wearing.

"I know, it's an ugly color," she said.

"Huh?"

"This sweater. But my mother gave it to me and I have to wear it once in a while."

He was still staring at her with a puzzled expression.

"I don't like pink either," she added.

"How did you know I don't like pink?" he asked.

"You must have told me," she replied.

He shook his head, but now she was distracted by the sight of the teacher coming into the classroom.

Mr. Henderson didn't *look* like a beast. In fact, he was a pretty ordinary looking man, average size, with wispy brown hair, glasses, and a bland expression. He certainly wasn't *feeling* bland, though. He was angry.

I can't believe they've doubled my class size! How am I supposed to teach forty kids? This is insane! And these new students are going to be just as stupid as the old ones. I've al-

ready got the worst eighth-grade group. And if their test scores don't go up, I'm never going to win the California Teacher of the Year award.

Had Mr. Henderson just said that out loud? Amy looked around. The lack of reaction on her classmates' faces told her that wasn't possible. Yet she knew this was exactly what he was thinking.

Just like she knew that Chris didn't like the color pink. And that the lady in the cafeteria didn't like the students.

"Open your textbooks to page eighty-two."

That was what Mr. Henderson said. But what he thought was *There's got to be some sort of rule about this. A restriction on class sizes. I'm calling the union.*

Amy started to shake. Something was very, very wrong. Was she sick? No, that wasn't possible—she was never sick. Well, hardly ever. She tried to pull herself together and listen to what the teacher was saying.

"Look carefully at the diagram at the top of the page. Who can tell us what this represents?" *No one. Because you're all too stupid. Wait, there's a hand going up. But he'll give the wrong answer. I don't know why I bothered to ask.*

Slowly, Amy raised her hand.

"Yes? What does the diagram represent?"

"I—I don't know. Can I be excused to go to the clinic, please? I'm not feeling very well."

Still expressionless, Mr. Henderson handed her a hall pass. As Amy made her way to the door, she could hear him asking someone to help him hand out pencils. He was wondering if he had enough for this huge class. But he wasn't telling them that, he was thinking it.

Amy walked quickly down the silent hall toward the school offices. What was she going to tell the school nurse when she reached the clinic? How could she explain what was going on in her head?

"Amy! Are you okay? You look so weird!"

Thank goodness, it was an actual speaking voice. Jan, also gripping a hall pass, was just coming out of the rest room.

"Um, I kind of have a headache," Amy said. It wasn't true, but it was the closest she could come to the truth—whatever the truth was. "Listen, Jan, there's something I need to tell you."

"What?"

"You better go to the mall right after school if you really want that jacket. There's only one left in your size."

Jan was clearly surprised. "How did you know I wanted to buy a jacket?"

"Didn't you tell me?"

"No. I was just thinking about it. And how do you know there's only one left in my size?"

Now Amy was having trouble catching her breath. "I—I don't know. I don't know!"

She didn't even bother to stop by the clinic. With her heart pounding and her head spinning, she ran out of the school.

f5ve

Even in her panic, when she arrived home, Amy was relieved that her mother wasn't there. It saved her from having to provide an explanation for something she couldn't explain. What would she have said?

"Hi, Mom, guess what? I left school early because I'm hearing things and I think I've got brain damage. Or maybe I'm having a mental breakdown. Or both."

No, she couldn't tell her mother anything like that. Nancy Candler would only go into her own version of panic—she'd call Dr. Dave, the two of them would haul Amy into the hospital, secret tests would be run, and Amy would be stuck there like a prisoner until some cure could be found. No thanks. Been there, done that. When she went crazy and collapsed, she'd do it in her own home.

Anyway, she didn't feel *sick,* like she did the time she had her ears pierced. A quick look in the mirror assured her that she didn't *look* weird either, like she had on the morning of her thirteenth birthday. She wasn't dizzy, she didn't feel like throwing up, and she didn't hurt.

But even so, she decided to treat herself like a sick person—at least, the way normal people behaved when they were sick. If she was going to be worried and frightened, at least she could be comfortable.

So she warmed up some soup in the microwave and put on a pair of old favorite pajamas, faded flannel ones printed with daisies. Then she curled up on the sofa with her soup, a quilt, and the remote control.

She felt a little calmer. There were no voices, and she had no idea what she'd find on TV. Of course, it was pretty much the same junk that had been on the last time she'd stayed home from school. Soap operas and game shows. And lots of commercials, mostly about job-training programs and retirement communities. She settled on good old reliable MTV. The video of the moment featured Eminem, not one of her favorite performers. She wouldn't want to know what *he* was really thinking.

Was that what had happened to her? she wondered. Had she'd turned into some kind of mind reader? Maybe that bolt of lightning on the beach had triggered some bizarre reaction in her brain. She had no idea what happened to ordinary people who were hit by lightning. She supposed it could have some impact on their brains. Maybe they became hyper, or forgot how to ride a bicycle or something. But she wasn't ordinary, and she certainly didn't have an ordinary brain. There was no way to predict what lightning would do to *her*.

Amy consoled herself with the thought that the effects were probably temporary. One of the soap operas she watched during school breaks featured a character who'd lived through a car accident. She'd hit her head, and when she woke up in the hospital she didn't know who she was. Then, about a year later, she was in another accident and got her memory back. Amy hoped she wouldn't have to wait for another bolt of lightning before she stopped hearing voices.

After a couple of hours of channel surfing, Amy felt perfectly normal. She rationalized that Chris must have told her once that he didn't like pink, so she'd just assumed he didn't like her sweater. And after all the horror stories she'd heard about Mr. Henderson, she'd just imagined him thinking about how he didn't like students. To think that Tasha had once accused her of not having any imagination! Maybe Amy's imagination was getting better with age.

Comforted by such thoughts, Amy began to feel ashamed of how she'd run out of school in a panic. She'd have to come up with some excuse to explain her odd behavior to her classmates tomorrow.

Actually, she'd have to think of some sort of explanation *now*, to give Tasha. From the window, she could see her friend coming up the walk.

"Are you okay?" Tasha asked anxiously when Amy opened the door. "Why did you run out of class?"

Unfortunately, Amy's new vivid imagination didn't provide her with anything original to say in response. "I had a headache" was all she came up with.

Tasha was suspicious. "You don't get headaches. You're too healthy."

Amy pretended to be offended. "For crying out loud, Tasha, I was struck by lightning two days ago! I think I'm entitled to have a little headache."

Tasha didn't look convinced, but fortunately she was too excited about other news to press the issue. "Guess what?" she said. "Peter asked me to go to the movies with him!"

"That's great!" Amy squealed. "See, I told you he liked you! And he doesn't think you're fat!"

Tasha beamed. "Yeah, I still can't believe it. How did you know that, anyway?"

"Just a feeling," Amy said.

"But you don't even know Peter, really. How could you guess he liked me?"

"It's not important," Amy said impatiently. "Now, tell me exactly how it happened and what he said."

Tasha regaled her with the tale, without omitting any details, not even the fact that Peter had stared over her head and shifted his weight from one foot to the other as he spoke.

"Yeah, that's how Eric was the first time he asked me for a date," Amy remembered. "I think it's a guy thing."

"He asked me if Eric was my brother," Tasha recalled. "He heard that Eric was the only tenth grader on the varsity basketball team. He *loves* basketball." She laughed. "I've never before been so grateful to have Eric for a brother. He gave us something to talk about."

Tasha's big date wasn't the only event Amy had missed that afternoon. There was other news worth reporting.

"You know that nasty woman in the cafeteria? The one who looks like she hates us? Well, it turns out she really does! She wanted to kill us! With poison!"

Amy faltered. "How—how do you know that?"

"She told Mr. Moore, that man in the wheelchair who runs the kitchen. She actually asked him if we'd be able to taste rat poison in meat loaf! Of course, Mr. Moore reported her to the principal. She claimed she was just joking, but Dr. Noble said she had a bad attitude. I guess people have complained about her before. Anyway, she was fired." Tasha gazed at Amy curiously. "Why are you looking so upset? You didn't like her either."

"I'm not upset," Amy replied automatically. "Um, what movie are you going to see with Peter?"

While Tasha chattered about the pros and cons of comedies versus scary movies, Amy tried to persuade herself that the cafeteria worker story was just another coincidence in a day that had been unusually filled with coincidences. She'd almost convinced herself that this was true when the phone rang.

"Hello?"

"Amy, hi, this is Jan. I'm calling from the mall. I just wanted to say thank you!"

"For what?" Amy asked, though she had a sinking suspicion she knew what Jan was about to tell her.

"You were right about the jacket. I got the last one in my size!"

Amy's stomach turned over. When she got off the phone, Tasha was staring at her.

"You're white as a ghost!"

"I *feel* like a ghost," Amy said. "Well, maybe not a ghost, but something spooky like that. Tasha, you're not going to believe this."

"Try me," Tasha advised. "You've told me a lot of unbelievable things before."

Amy tried to put it into words. "Ever since I was struck by lightning, something weird has been going on in my head. I thought I was hearing voices, but that's not it, exactly. It's like I'm reading people's minds. I know what they're thinking."

Tasha was intrigued. "Oh yeah?" She closed her eyes. "What number am I thinking of right now?"

"Tasha, it's not a magic trick!" Amy declared hotly. "It's scary! It just happens once in a while, I don't know why or how. And there's more. I—I think I can see what's going to happen sometimes."

Tasha gasped. "You mean, like a fortune-teller?"

"Maybe—I'm not sure," Amy said. "Sometimes things just come to me." She told Tasha about Jan's jacket. And how she knew they'd be in the same math class, that there would be meat loaf for lunch, and that

Peter was going to ask for a date. "I suppose they could all be coincidences," she added.

But Tasha didn't think so. "Amy, this is incredible! You can see into the future!"

"Well, yeah, but—"

"You can predict stuff! And mind reading, wow! You'll know when a boy likes you, or when someone's telling a lie. That's so cool!"

"You think so?" Amy asked doubtfully.

"I *know* so! Amy, you'll know test questions in advance! How far into the future can you see?"

"I'm not sure," Amy said. "I haven't figured out what kind of stuff I know."

Tasha was getting more and more worked up. "Maybe you'll be able to predict earthquakes and hurricanes, all kinds of natural disasters. Amy, you could save people's lives!"

Amy hadn't considered this possibility. "I don't know if it works like that," she said, but the prospect was certainly interesting.

Now Tasha was staring at the TV screen. "And you could make a lot of money! Look!"

Amy looked at the TV. A glamorous woman with a big smile was speaking.

"Do you want to know what's going to happen to you and your family?" the woman said. "Of course you

44

do! Well, now you *can*! You can talk to a real psychic! Just call this number. Your first three minutes are absolutely free!"

"They get you hooked with the three free minutes, then I'll bet they charge you a fortune," Tasha declared.

"Oh, come on, Tasha, it's a big fake," Amy said. "Everyone knows that. They don't have any real fortune-telling skill, they just tell people what they want to hear."

"Yeah, I know, they're all phonies," Tasha agreed. "But *you're* not. What you've got, it's real! Isn't it?" Her eyes were bright with excitement.

Amy nodded. "It looks that way."

Then she realized that her panic had disappeared. And *she* was feeling some stirrings of excitement too.

s**i**x**6**

Amy approached the subject casually and carefully with her mother the next morning at breakfast. "Mom, do you believe that some people can see into the future?" she asked.

Nancy considered the question. "Well, there are sociologists and economists who try to predict situations, based on statistics and their previous experiences. A broker, for example, might be able to make an educated guess as to whether the stock market will go up or down. A meteorologist can study weather patterns and know that there's a likelihood of rain in the near future."

Amy shook her head. "No, no, I'm not talking about those kinds of predictions. I mean people with a psychic gift. People who just know what's going to happen."

Her mother gazed at her reprovingly. "Amy, I'm a scientist. I don't believe in crystal balls and tarot cards."

"But what if someone suddenly started thinking that certain things would happen, and then they *did* happen?"

"Pure coincidence," Nancy said.

"But what if it wasn't coincidence?" Amy persisted. "What if it happened over and over again, and the person was always right?"

Now Nancy was looking at her with a tinge of suspicion in her eyes. "Amy, are we talking about someone you know?"

"Of course not," Amy said quickly. "I'm just reading a book about a girl who can tell the future."

"And it's fiction, right? It's not a true story."

"That's right," Amy said. "It's fiction." She didn't like to lie to her mother, and she wasn't much good at it anyway, but fortunately her mother didn't sense any real danger in what she was saying. And then the doorbell rang, which provided a distraction.

"That's Tasha, I've gotta go. Bye, Mom." She tossed

48

a hasty kiss in her mother's direction and ran out of the kitchen. Tasha hit her with a question before she could get the front door closed behind her.

"What do you think I had for breakfast this morning?"

Amy hazarded a guess. "Something dietetic?"

"Amy! Can't you read my mind?"

Amy reprimanded her. "Tasha, don't ask me to read your mind like that. I don't want to fool around with this mind reading and fortune-telling business. It's not a game."

"Oh, come on, just this once," Tasha pleaded. "I'll think about what I ate, and you tell me what I'm thinking." She closed her eyes tightly.

Amy sighed. "Okay, just this once." She concentrated, and an image appeared in her head. "Special K cereal."

"Wow!" Tasha was impressed. "There's no way you could have just guessed that. I only just started eating Special K today because it's supposed to be healthy. What did Eric eat?" She closed her eyes again.

"Tasha!"

"Okay, okay." They started walking. "But for your information, he had raspberry Pop-Tarts. I could smell them, and I didn't even ask for a bite. Don't I have incredible willpower?"

"I hope so," Amy said. "Because there're going to be glazed doughnuts at lunch today."

"Hey, you said you wouldn't play games," Tasha accused her.

"I was thinking about lunch and it just came to me," Amy told her. "I figured I should warn you, so you'd be prepared." She knew Tasha had a particular weakness for glazed doughnuts.

"Glazed doughnuts, huh? Are you sure about that? We've never had glazed doughnuts in the cafeteria before." Tasha sighed. "Will they be warm?"

"I'm not going to concentrate on details," Amy declared. "I shouldn't even be thinking about lunch. I have to take this gift seriously. I don't know how long it's going to last. And maybe it will wear off if I use it too much. I need to save my predictions and mind reading for important stuff."

"But it's so much fun to know the little things," Tasha said wistfully.

She was right—it *was* fun, and it was very hard for Amy not to let herself enjoy the gift. She had to give in to the temptation every now and then. For example, when Alan Greenfield came tearing into their homeroom seconds after the bell rang and Ms. Weller glared at him fiercely, Amy had no difficulty understanding why. She knew that Alan already had four demerits for tardiness, and one more would mean a whole week of detention.

"I'm sorry, Ms. Weller," he said breathlessly. "But there was an accident near my house, and my dad was stuck in traffic, and that's why I'm late. Really, you can call him and he'll tell you that's the truth."

Only it wasn't the truth. Amy didn't even have to concentrate to know this. Alan had overslept, as usual. And his father was out of town and couldn't be reached.

Amy marveled at how easy it was to know that someone was lying. It was neat, being the only one who could know what was really going on in someone's head. Like when Simone asked Linda what she thought of her new spiky haircut and Linda said it was fabulous. It took Amy very little effort to know that Linda really thought Simone looked like a porcupine.

And it was cool to know that while Ms. Weller was calling the roll, the teacher was actually thinking about how her new shoes were killing her. Not to mention that Amy sensed what was going to be included in the morning announcements. When she heard the girl behind her moaning about how she would have to miss soccer practice that afternoon to get her braces tightened and the coach would kill her because this would be her third absence, Amy couldn't resist the opportunity to relieve her anxiety.

"Don't worry, soccer practice is canceled this afternoon," Amy told her.

The girl was surprised to hear this from Amy. "How do *you* know? You're not on the soccer team."

"Oh, I just have a feeling," Amy replied loftily.

Sure enough, among the morning announcements over the intercom was word that girls' soccer practice had been canceled because a large patch of poison ivy had been discovered—*just minutes earlier*. Amy could feel the soccer girl's curious eyes on her.

Stop it, Amy warned herself. You're doing exactly what you told Tasha you wouldn't do—you're making a game out of this. You're showing off. But she was tempted again when she noticed Layne frantically scribbling in her notebook and looking unusually anxious. Amy could easily have asked Layne why she was upset, but instead she probed Layne's head. Then she knew that Layne had left an essay at home that was due in her history class today, and she was trying to rewrite it in time to hand it in next period.

Amy nudged her. "Your history teacher's absent. The essays won't be collected till tomorrow."

Layne was taken aback. "How do you know?"

This time, Amy came up with a plausible explanation. "I was in the office this morning, and I heard the secretary talking to her."

"*Him*," Layne corrected. "I've got Mr. Abernathy for history."

"Well, that's who the secretary was talking to," Amy insisted. "So you don't have to rewrite the essay."

"Okay," Layne said. "Thanks for telling me. That's a relief." But she was looking more puzzled than ever.

Now Amy was really annoyed with herself. She had to stop this at once. Rumors would start, and she would have some serious explaining to do. It wasn't as if people were forcing their thoughts on her—she was beginning to realize that her mind reading and fortune-telling had to be turned on somehow. It wasn't automatic.

But it was awfully easy. After homeroom, when she passed Mr. Henderson in the hall, she couldn't resist a little peek into his head. This time, she learned something *really* interesting—and useful. There was going to be a pop quiz in math that afternoon.

She'd tell Tasha, of course. There was no way she'd keep vital information like this from her best friend. And there was someone else she wanted to inform.

She knew that Chris had his first-period class right across the hall from hers, and she found him already there. He was alone in the classroom, slumped in his seat, aimlessly tapping a pencil on his desk. He greeted her with a nod and just the hint of a smile.

She tried to ignore the bad vibes she was getting from him. "Big news," she told him. "Pop quiz in math today."

She waited for him to ask the usual question—"How do you know?"—but it didn't come. "Okay" was all he said.

His eyes were bleak. But this time, Amy used some willpower—and instead of reading his mind, she tried to find out in the normal way what was bothering him. "Chris, what's going on? I can tell something's wrong."

He acted like he didn't know what she was talking about. "Nothing's going on. Everything's fine."

"Oh, come on, Chris," she said impatiently. "It's written all over your face. Something's bugging you. I wish you'd tell me; maybe I could help." When he didn't respond, she took a deep breath. "Is it me? Am I bugging you?"

He shook his head. "No, it's not you. Well, maybe it is, in a way. I mean, it's got something to do with you."

She gulped. "Any chance you could be a little more specific?"

A couple of students had drifted in. Chris lowered his voice. "I think I'm getting sent to a foster home."

"Oh." Amy didn't know what to say. "I guess that's pretty scary, huh?"

"No kidding."

"But it might be okay," she added. "It might even be nice. And it's got to be better than living in a homeless shelter, right?"

"Not necessarily," he said. "Even if it's nice, it's no good. See, it's not around here."

Amy felt a twinge in her heart. "Where is it?"

"Some suburb about an hour from here. I'd be going to a different school. And some foster families, they keep a pretty tight rein on kids. I won't be able to see you much."

The twinge had turned into a real pain. "Oh" was all she could say again. This was something she hadn't expected. She hated the way Chris was all stressed out, and she didn't particularly like the way she was feeling either. She was going to have to give in to temptation again.

More kids were coming into the room, and Amy had to get across the hall to her own class. She spoke quickly. "Don't worry. You won't be shipped off to some foster home in the suburbs. It's not going to happen."

He gave her an odd look. "You planning to take over the city's welfare system?"

The bell was about to ring. "We'll talk after math. Don't forget about the pop quiz!"

She ran out, leaving behind a very confused Chris.

seven

"I told Peter about the pop quiz," Tasha whispered to Amy as they waited in the cafeteria line. "He's going to spread the word."

"You didn't tell him how you learned about it, did you?" Amy asked.

"I just said it was a rumor," Tasha assured her. "That I heard from you," she added.

"Oh, great," Amy groaned. "Now everyone will want to know where I heard it. Hey, when are you having your big date with Peter?"

"Saturday," Tasha said. "He's such a gentleman! He's going to pick me up at home instead of just meeting me at the movie. And he said that if my parents didn't want me to go out alone with a boy, I could invite my brother to come along. As if! But it was sweet of him to suggest that, don't you think?"

"I guess," Amy said doubtfully, though it seemed kind of weird to her. Peter didn't strike her as the kind of person who would be overly concerned with someone's parents. But then again, she really didn't know him.

A faint aroma tickled her nose. "You smell that?"

"What?" But a few steps closer to the counter, Tasha caught the scent as well. "Ohmigod, you were right. Glazed doughnuts. Oh, Amy, how am I going to deal with glazed doughnuts?"

A sweet-faced woman who was serving up the food looked at Tasha in dismay. "Don't you like glazed doughnuts, dear?"

"I *love* glazed doughnuts," Tasha moaned. "But I'm on a diet!"

The woman smiled. "Well, one little doughnut won't kill you. There's really not that much sugar in them. I know, because I made them myself."

"You did?" Amy was surprised. "I didn't know food was actually cooked here. I thought it came in trucks and just got heated up."

"That's true," the woman replied. "But glazed dough-nuts are my specialty, and I wanted to make them on my first day here. As a special treat."

"That's nice," Amy said. "Thank you, Ms. Robertson."

"You're welcome!"

"You knew her name!" Tasha squealed in Amy's ear. "You've never seen her before, have you?"

"No," Amy said. "But that was an easy one. She's wearing a name tag."

"Oh. Well, at least she's nicer than that last lady." Tasha gazed wistfully at the doughnut on her plate as she set the tray on the table. "I'll bet her doughnuts are good too."

Amy took a bite of hers. "Not bad."

"Are you going to eat that in front of me?" Tasha wailed in agony. Then she saw Peter approaching them and brightened. "Hi, Peter, want my doughnut?"

"Sure," he said, and Tasha looked relieved as she got rid of the temptation on her plate. "Hey, did you ask your parents about Saturday?"

"Yes, they said it's fine," Tasha told him. "And I don't need to bring my brother with us."

"Oh. Okay." He turned to Amy. "Are you sure about that math quiz today? 'Cause if it's for real, I'm going to go cram."

Amy studied her food. She didn't want to meet Peter's eyes or know what he was thinking. "Yeah, I guess. I mean, that's what I heard."

"It's for real," Tasha broke in. "Absolutely, positively. I crammed all last period."

Peter accepted that. "Okay, see you in class."

"You shouldn't have said that," Amy scolded Tasha. "He'll want to know how we could be so sure."

But Peter wasn't the only one she needed to worry about. Seconds later, Jan appeared at their table. She got right to the point.

"How did you know there's going to be a pop quiz?" she asked Amy.

Amy tried to be offhand. "Oh, it's just an educated guess."

"No, it isn't," Jan said. "You *know*! Just like you knew about my jacket. You're psychic, Amy Candler!"

"Shhh," Amy hissed. "Keep your voice down!"

"It's true, isn't it?" Jan said excitedly. "I always thought there was something different about you, Amy. Now I know what it is. You have visions, you see things!"

Amy tried to argue. "You don't really believe in that stuff, Jan, do you?"

"Of course I do! You wouldn't believe what I've learned from Ouija boards and palm readers. And I'm not the only one. My father says that sometimes the police department consults psychics to find out about crimes!"

Amy was weakening. "Really? The police believe in psychic powers?"

"Lots of people do," Tasha interjected. "I have an aunt whose friend does astrological forecasts. She gets paid for telling the future! This isn't something to be ashamed of, Amy. You should be proud of this talent!"

Amy's shoulders slumped. Now Tasha had really done it. She'd confirmed Jan's suspicions, and soon the word would spread all over school: Amy Candler was a psychic.

"Jan, don't tell anyone, okay?" Amy pleaded. But that was a ridiculous request. How could she expect anyone to keep a secret like that?

The word was already getting around. She could feel it when she went into the math class, where most students were frantically perusing their textbooks. Everyone seemed to know she was the source of the pop-quiz rumor. Resolutely, she forced herself not to get any deeper into their heads.

The bell rang, and Mr. Henderson spoke. "Close your books. We're having a pop quiz." His brow furrowed slightly when this announcement wasn't greeted with moans and groans, but he didn't say anything about it. He handed out papers and pencils. "You have thirty minutes to complete the problems."

All the students bent their heads over the papers and began scribbling. The problems weren't difficult, Amy thought. Anyone who had done their homework the night before shouldn't have any difficulty. Amy decided that knowing about the test beforehand really hadn't helped anyone—it just made them less nervous. And anyway, it wasn't like she'd told them exactly what would be *on* the quiz.

She finished early and looked at Chris, who was still working. He looked pale and tense, but Amy knew that wasn't because of the test. He was thinking about his future.

So was Amy. She was seeing him in a home with overly attentive foster parents who watched his every move and questioned his every action. But was that the real future she was seeing, or his own fears of what the future might bring?

It didn't matter, she decided, because it wasn't going to happen. She wouldn't let it happen. She was smart—she could come up with a solution to his predicament.

She thought about what Chris had told her about the shelter system. It seemed pretty chaotic, like no one really knew what anyone else was doing. People came and went, records weren't kept, and the staff was constantly changing. That was why a minor like Chris had been able to hang out in an adult men's shelter. No one had paid any attention to him. Until now.

Okay, so maybe there was one conscientious and idealistic worker at the shelter. But there were other shelters. And if the system was so messy, Chris could take advantage of it.

It wasn't that hard to come up with a plan of action for him. Once that was done, she entertained herself by gazing around the room and exploring a few minds. It was interesting to discover that Rafe Donato had a massive crush on Carrie Nolan, who sat in front of him. He was trying to get up the nerve to ask her to go to the movies this weekend. Amy wondered if Carrie knew about Rafe's feelings.

So she poked around and learned that yes, Carrie knew, but she wasn't happy about it. She had absolutely no interest in Rafe. And if Rafe asked her out, Carrie would say no, and she wouldn't lie to spare his feelings. Carrie believed in total honesty, which meant that Rafe was going to get hurt, big-time.

Amy wished she didn't know this. Rafe was sweet and kind of shy. He was small for his age, which probably made him feel insecure. It saddened Amy to know he'd be rejected, and she wished she could warn him to forget about Carrie.

She shifted her attention to Danny Eckhart, one of the snottiest guys in the eighth grade. He hung out in the most popular crowd and thought he was totally cool. What did a guy like that think about?

Right now he was thinking about a belated birthday gift that was supposed to arrive today with his visiting godmother. He didn't care about his godmother, but he was looking forward to the gift. The godmother was pretty wealthy, and he thought he'd be getting an envelope stuffed with cash.

With a little effort, she directed her mind to see what the godmother was bringing Danny. She couldn't help grinning. Danny would be getting an envelope, but not stuffed with cash. The birthday present was a gift certificate—to a bookstore. And Danny wasn't the kind of guy who'd be thrilled with a gift of books. This was fun!

Amy turned to Michelle Unser, another member of the popular crowd. Immediately, she had a vision of Michelle in a hospital bed. *That* wasn't pleasant. Amy shifted to the girl sitting next to Michelle. Amy didn't know her name, but she had a clear image of the girl crying, hard. Amy didn't want to know why.

This was *not* fun. Thank goodness, Henderson distracted her by calling for the papers. Concentrating on class for the rest of the period kept her from thinking about her fellow students.

As soon as class was over, she beckoned to Chris. "I have an idea," she told him. "A way to keep you out of the foster home. Meet me after school on the steps."

He agreed readily. But then Jan practically pushed him aside. "Okay, my turn. Am I going to win the junior tennis tournament this year?"

"Jan!" Amy looked around anxiously to make sure others hadn't heard. "Not now!"

"Okay, I'll meet you on the steps after school," Jan said, and took off.

Amy sighed. She really wanted to have a private talk with Chris after school. She hoped Jan wouldn't linger and bug her with a million questions.

As it turned out, it wasn't only Jan she had to deal with. When Amy arrived on the steps after school, she was dismayed to see Jan accompanied by Michelle Unser and a girl Amy didn't know. They all wanted their fortunes told.

Amy was extremely uncomfortable. "Listen, guys, I don't know if this really works. I mean, I've been getting some visions, but I don't know if they just happen automatically or not."

"Well, just try," Jan said. "Think about me playing tennis. Concentrate. Now, picture the big tournament in Van Nuys. Do you get any visions of me being the winner?"

Amy tried to oblige. And in her mind, a picture began to form. A tennis court . . . Jan and some other girl on opposite sides of the net. The ball going back and forth. Jan swinging, missing, the other girl throwing her racket in the air . . . a big gold trophy in the arms of the other girl.

"I don't think you're going to win, Jan."

Jan was shocked. "Are you serious? I've been practicing, three hours every day! I've been winning every match!"

"I'm sorry," Amy said lamely. "But I see someone else with the trophy." To her alarm, Jan's eyes filled with tears. "Look, I could be wrong," she said hastily.

Jan sniffled, wiped her eyes, and turned to Michelle. "Your turn."

"Is my mother going to let me go on a ski trip this weekend?" Michelle asked.

Amy concentrated. Yes, she could definitely see Michelle careening down a snowy mountain. But then she saw something else—and she knew why she'd had that earlier vision of Michelle in a hospital bed.

66

"She's going to let you go, but maybe you shouldn't. Because you'll break your leg."

Michelle looked at her in disbelief. "No way. I'm an excellent skier."

Amy shrugged. "That's what I see."

"You sound like my mother," Michelle declared. "I don't think you're a real psychic." She turned to the other girl. "Come on, let's get out of here."

"Wait," the other girl said. "I want to ask something. Is my grandfather going to be all right?"

"Your grandfather?" Amy repeated.

"Yes, he's in the hospital. Will he recover?"

The girl clearly loved her grandfather. Amy could see that without even exploring her thoughts. Then she had a vision . . . a church, a coffin, this girl sobbing . . .

"Well?" the girl asked. "What do you see?"

"Nothing," Amy said. "I'm—I'm not getting any visions."

"You see?" Michelle said. "She's a fake, just like those TV psychics. Let's get out of here." The two girls linked arms and walked away.

Jan spoke sadly. "I kind of hope they're right, Amy. I really want to win that championship."

Chris joined them on the steps. "Hi, what's up?"

"Amy's telling futures," Jan said. "She thinks she's got a psychic gift."

"I never said that, Jan!" Amy exclaimed. "It's you and Tasha who keep saying I can see the future!"

"Amy, you're just going to have to accept your gift," Jan declared. "Just like I'm going to have to accept the fact that I won't be a tennis champion." A tear trickled down her face. "Excuse me," she mumbled, and ran off.

Chris stared after her. Then he turned to Amy. "Hey, is this true? Can you see what's going to happen?"

Amy sighed. "It sort of feels like that." She told Chris about the visions she'd been having.

Chris was impressed. "Cool," he said. "So read my future. Am I going to a foster home?"

Amy pulled herself together. "Not if you don't want to. Come on, let's go talk."

e**8**ght

"Fish sticks," Amy told Tasha as they walked to school the next morning. "And peas. Tomato salad." Her brow puckered. "And I'm seeing glazed doughnuts again."

"No way," Tasha objected. "School lunches never contain the same food two days in a row. I think it's against the law or something. You're confusing the future with the past."

Amy considered this. "I could be losing the gift already," she said.

"Geez, I hope not!" Tasha cried in alarm. "I've got so many questions for you! You have to tell me if I'm going to be a famous writer someday. And if I'm going to get married, and how many kids I'll have, all that kind of stuff. Oh, and if the dentist is going to find any cavities when I go for my checkup next week, and—"

"Whoa!" Amy broke in. "I'm not a machine, Tasha! And don't be so greedy! Like I told you, I don't know how this thing works. I might have only a few predictions left. And if we don't get glazed doughnuts again today, I'll know it's starting to mess up. Because I'm getting a very clear picture of the lunch trays in my head."

"Well, let's not waste your talent with lunch predictions," Tasha said hastily. "And seriously, Amy, I think you ought to charge people. Why give your gift away for free? You could make some real money!"

That wasn't a bad idea, Amy thought. She didn't receive a fortune in allowance each week, and she didn't have a regular baby-sitting job or any other way to make extra cash. On the other hand, she seriously doubted that many people would truly believe she could tell fortunes.

She was wrong. As they approached Parkside Middle School, she noted that there seemed to be a lot more people than usual gathered on the front steps. And most of them turned out to be waiting for *her*.

Clearly, the Parkside rumor mill had been churning

at top speed. She didn't even know most of the kids waiting to see her.

Tasha was thrilled. "Tell them it's a dollar a question. No, a dollar fifty."

But Amy was having second thoughts about charging. "I think I should do freebies today," she told Tasha. "Until I'm absolutely, positively sure everything comes true."

"Just until lunch," Tasha proposed. "If there are doughnuts, you start making them pay."

Amy faced the clamoring crowd on the steps. "Listen, you guys, I don't know how this works, and I might not—"

She didn't get any farther. A tall, blond girl moved to the front, and no one objected. Amy didn't know her, but she recognized the girl immediately—Lorna Leaver, the most popular girl in the ninth grade. Captain of the cheerleading squad, part-time model, and finalist in the California Junior Miss All-American Sweetheart beauty pageant last year. Her question was abrupt and to the point.

"Will I win California Junior Miss All-American Sweetheart next month?" she demanded.

Amy took in the girl's beautiful features and perfect figure, and immediately an image formed in her mind. A crown on her head, roses in her arms, a banner across her chest—but the banner didn't read California Junior Miss All-American Sweetheart.

"Oh, wow!" she said.

"What?"

"I don't see All-American Sweetheart," Amy began, but before the girl's face could fall, she announced, "You're going to be Miss America! In ten years!"

Lorna didn't look the least bit surprised. "Thanks," she said, and walked away.

The next one was almost as easy. A boy wanted to know if he'd ever win an Olympic medal for swimming. Amy concentrated and saw a picture of him in a group, under an Olympic banner. She was about to say yes when she realized that this particular boy didn't have a medal around his neck and another boy did.

"You'll be on the team," she said. "But I don't see a medal."

His face fell. "Are you *sure*?"

"It's just what I see," Amy hastened to say. "Maybe you'll be on the team twice, and the first time you won't win and the next time you will." But as hard as she tried, she couldn't picture a medal around his neck.

The boy seemed relieved, though. "Okay, as long as I win a medal eventually. Will it be a gold medal?"

"I can't tell," Amy lied. "The images aren't in color."

The next person asked about marriage and children, and Amy was happy to tell him there would be a wife and three kids someday. A girl asked if she would become a doctor, and Amy had no difficulty seeing her in a white coat with a stethoscope around her neck. The next girl wanted to know if she would ever date one of the Backstreet Boys. Amy had to tell her no.

She was beginning to relax and enjoy herself. It was kind of fun being the center of attention! For ages, her mother had warned her never to show off—it could be dangerous if the wrong people found out about her genetic structure. But this was different, she reasoned. There was no evidence that her new talent had anything to do with being a clone. Anyone who'd been lucky enough to get struck by that lightning would probably be telling futures now.

The next request came from a group of three. They wanted to know the questions on an upcoming history test. Amy hesitated. As she was considering the ethics of this one, Peter passed by on his way up the stairs and waved at Tasha.

"Is he thinking about me?" Tasha asked Amy in a whisper.

Amy looked away from the history group and glanced at Peter. She was only able to get a glimpse before he disappeared into the building. "All I can get from his mind is basketball," she whispered back to Tasha.

Tasha nodded understandingly. "The Lakers won last night."

"Hey, what about the test?" one of the three demanded.

Amy made a decision. "I can't answer that kind of question. It's cheating."

The group grumbled and looked disappointed, but they didn't press the issue. The next candidate was a petite, slender girl with a heart-shaped face. She was young, probably just a seventh grader, and she gazed at Amy in awe.

Amy spoke kindly. "Yes? How can I help you?"

"It's about ballet," the girl said nervously. "I'm trying out for *The Nutcracker* next week. Will I be chosen?"

Amy started to conjure up Parkside's next Christmas presentation of *The Nutcracker* when she was distracted by Mr. Henderson coming up the steps. "It's almost time for the bell," he warned them.

Amy took the opportunity to take a quick peek at his thoughts.

Amazing, the way those scores went up. I didn't expect it to work so fast. I just might end up being teacher of the year after all. But maybe it's just a fluke. . . .

It must refer to his teaching methods, Amy thought. Then she thought she heard his mind contemplating another quiz today, to see if the students were really improving.

"Well?"

Amy turned back to the young ballerina. "Huh?"

"Will I be in *The Nutcracker*?"

"No," Amy said.

"Come on, we'll be late," Tasha said, and grabbed Amy's arm. Along with the others on the steps, they ran into the building—but not before Amy caught a glimpse of the ballerina's crestfallen expression.

nine

Tasha was already in the cafeteria line when Amy arrived at lunchtime, and Amy knew immediately from the expression on Tasha's face that she'd made another correct prediction.

"Fish sticks, peas, tomatoes," Tasha told Amy in a voice filled with awe. "*And* glazed doughnuts."

"Glazed doughnuts *again*?" The boy standing behind Amy was surprised. "Two days in a row?"

Ms. Robertson, the nice lady behind the counter, beamed. "The students raved about my doughnuts to your principal yesterday," she told the kids in the line.

"So I asked Dr. Noble for permission to offer them regularly. And she said yes!"

Her announcement was greeted with applause. Personally, Amy hadn't thought the doughnuts were all that great—a little too sweet for her taste—and she doubted that students had actually raved to the school principal. But she had to admit, Ms. Robertson's specialty was better than most cafeteria desserts, like the purple gelatin stuff or the yellow goo or the caramel-colored lump with white spots. At least glazed doughnuts could be identified.

"Have you made any more predictions today?" Tasha asked as they sat down with their lunches.

"Nothing major," Amy told her. "I heard Simone saying she was going to get a tattoo, and I told her she shouldn't because it'll get infected."

"Did she believe you?"

"I hope so." Amy shuddered. "I could see this really disgusting scabby thing on her shoulder." She hesitated. "Something kind of creepy happened in homeroom."

"What?"

"You know Ms. Weller, my homeroom teacher? I was poking around her head, and I found out she's trying to adopt a baby. She's going to pay a ton of money to some agency to get a baby for her, from another country. She's really excited about this."

"Cool," Tasha commented.

"That's what I thought too," Amy said. "Until I started to wonder if the baby would be a boy or a girl, and whether or not Ms. Weller would stop teaching to take care of it. And you know what I saw? There won't be any baby. Something will go wrong, and she's going to be terribly upset."

Tasha was stricken. "How awful! Maybe you should tell her now, before she gets too involved."

"How can I do that?" Amy asked. "I don't want to crush her dreams. Anyway, I could be wrong."

"You weren't wrong about the glazed doughnuts," Tasha reminded her.

"You can't compare glazed doughnuts and babies," Amy said. She was distracted and pleased to see Chris coming into the cafeteria, and she waved.

"He doesn't come in here much, does he?" Tasha noted as he came toward them.

"That's because he doesn't have money for food," Amy told her. "He usually skips out at lunch and goes back to the shelter, where he can get a free sandwich and soup."

But he wouldn't be going back to a shelter today, and

for a good reason. "I did what you said," he told Amy. "Last night I got my stuff together and I went looking for a new shelter."

"And did you find one?" she asked. She noticed that his eyes were puffy, like he hadn't had much sleep.

He nodded. "It's farther from here, so I can't go back for lunch. It's noisy too, because it's a lot bigger. But I guess that's good. The bigger it is, the more disorganized it'll be, and no one will pay any attention to me."

"But what are you going to do about lunch?" Amy asked in dismay. "You're going to starve!" She took Tasha's doughnut and her own, wrapped them in the paper napkin, and handed the little package to Chris. He shook his head.

"I'm not going to take your food away," he said.

"We don't want the doughnuts," Amy said. "Tasha's on a diet and they're too sweet for me."

"How can anything be *too* sweet?" Tasha muttered, but she agreed with Amy's offer. "Take them," she told Chris. "Otherwise they'll just get thrown away."

He eyed the doughnuts hungrily. "Well, if you're just going to toss them in the garbage . . ."

Jan approached them with Luke Simmons. "Amy, Luke needs to know something."

The boy looked a little embarrassed, but he asked

his question. "I'm thinking about running for student body president in the spring," he confided. "But I don't want to run if I'm not going to win. I'd feel stupid. So, I want to know, if I run, will I win?"

Amy studied him for a minute. "No," she said regretfully. "You won't."

Luke's face fell, and Jan sighed. "Well, I guess it's better to know ahead of time. Amy, could you think again about my tennis championship? Are you *sure* I can't win?"

Amy nodded sadly. "That's what I see."

"I've got another question," Luke said suddenly. "What about my future? What am I going to be?"

Amy considered that. "A lawyer," she said finally.

Luke wasn't pleased with this answer either. "Not an astronaut? I've always wanted to be an astronaut!"

"Sorry," Amy said. "You're going to be a lawyer."

Now Luke's face went really dark, and Jan looked annoyed. "Gee, do you have to break *everybody's* heart, Amy? Let's go, Luke."

Amy stared after them in dismay. "I didn't mean to depress anyone."

"You're just telling them the truth," Tasha said briskly. "If they can't handle it, too bad for them. C'mon, it's time for class."

Amy, Tasha, and Chris headed for math. Peter was

standing just outside the door, and he greeted Tasha with a smile.

"I checked on the movie time for Saturday afternoon," he told her. "It's at two-fifteen, so I'll come by your place around one, okay?"

"Actually, I have a dentist appointment Saturday morning," Tasha replied. "It's right near the movie theater, so why don't I just meet you there?"

Amy thought Peter looked oddly disappointed, but he just shrugged and said, "Okay. But I'm taking you home afterward."

Tasha blushed slightly. "Sure, if you want to."

"I think he must really like her," Amy confided in Chris as they walked into the classroom.

Chris seemed surprised. "Yeah? In phys ed, he's always talking about Simone Cusack."

"Really?" Amy turned to look at Peter and Tasha coming in behind them. Peter grinned at her.

"Hey, what's going to happen in class? Henderson got any nasty tricks planned for us?"

Suddenly Amy remembered what she'd thought she heard in the teacher's head that morning, and she gasped. No, she had to have been mistaken. Nobody gave pop quizzes two days in a row.

Except for Mr. Henderson. They'd all just sat down

when he announced, "Close your books. We're having a pop quiz."

This time there were real groans. And more than a couple of people shot surprised looks at Amy. She slumped down in her seat. Surely everyone couldn't start expecting her to predict everything!

Mr. Henderson passed out his personal pencils and the quizzes. Amy scanned hers quickly. It didn't look any harder than yesterday's—different problems, of course, but the same type. Obviously, he was testing to make sure yesterday wasn't a fluke.

Amy finished her test quickly, then furtively examined her classmates. Were they mad at her for not telling them they were going to have another quiz? Had she just blown her reputation as a legitimate psychic?

She probed a couple of minds. Yes, she could definitely detect some bad feelings and doubts aimed in her direction. Her stomach churned in dismay. But when her radar hit Peter, she learned something even worse.

Too bad I can't pick her up at her house. I want to meet her brother. That's the only reason I asked her out to begin with. Eric Morgan is practically famous—he's the only tenth grader playing on a major high school team. I gotta get to know him. I gotta get him to practice with me. Bet he won't even be home when we get back there after the movie. What a bummer! How much time am I going to have to spend with Tasha just to know Eric? She's no babe, nothing like Simone.

Amy didn't want to hear any more. This was too, too depressing. He was just using Tasha so he could pal around with Eric. Tasha was going to be devastated when she found out. And of course, she'd want to know why Amy hadn't warned her. But if Amy *did* tell her—how could she stand being the bearer of such bad news?

Staring out the window, Amy tried to decide what to do. Vaguely, she noticed a man crossing the street in front of the school. Suddenly a horrific picture exploded in her head.

Now everyone, including Mr. Henderson, was looking at her, and she realized she must have shrieked. She didn't care. She leaped up from her seat and ran to the window.

"Stop! Stop!" she screamed.

Of course, the man couldn't hear her, not over the roar of the motorcycle that came speeding around the corner—and slammed right into him. The squeal of brakes and the sound of the motorcycle crashing into a car brought half the class to the window.

"Take your seats!" Henderson bellowed. "Everyone, sit down!"

But like Amy, they were glued to the awful sight. The man who had been crossing the street was now lying still in a pool of blood. The impact had sent the motorcyclist flying way down the road. He wasn't moving either. Another car swerved to miss him and crashed into a telephone pole. Now the air was pierced with the sounds of car alarms and sirens.

Amy felt sick. For the first time in a very, very long time, she thought she might actually throw up. She pushed aside the students who'd gathered behind her and ran out the door. Holding her breath, with a hand clapped over her mouth, she raced into the closest rest room. Once inside a stall, she knelt on the floor and leaned her head against the toilet seat.

The wave of nausea passed, but her head was throbbing. Was it physical? Was her brain reacting to the terrible premonition? Or was it an emotional response to what she'd seen? She couldn't be sure.

She couldn't possibly have stopped the accident— she knew that. There was no way she could have alerted the pedestrian in time. But maybe, just maybe, if she hadn't been so uptight about the way her classmates were thinking about her, about the way Peter was thinking about Tasha, she might have had the premonition earlier and been able to warn the man somehow.

"Amy? Are you in here?"

It was Tasha's voice. Amy came out of the stall. "Are you all right?" Tasha asked anxiously.

"Yeah," Amy said faintly. She went to a sink, turned on the cold water full blast, and began splashing her face. Her head began to clear. And then she became aware of another sound. A soft whimpering was coming from behind the door of another stall.

Tasha heard it too. She went to the door and rapped softly. "Hello?" she called. "You okay in there?"

The door opened, and a wan face looked out. Amy recognized her immediately—she was the seventh grader who wanted to be in *The Nutcracker*. The girl's eyes flickered from Tasha to Amy, then widened.

"Oh! Hi."

"Hi," Amy replied. "Look, I hope you're not still upset about what I told you this morning. I mean, I could have been wrong."

"That's okay," the girl said softly. "It's not the end of the world. There are so many people who try out, I knew there was a chance I wouldn't make it. The important thing is for me to just keep dancing. I'm going to be a real ballet dancer in a professional company someday." Her tone faltered. "Won't I?"

Amy stared at her. She wished she knew how she could stop the image that was forming in her head. She could see the future clearly, too clearly. The girl would be told she was too short for serious ballet, that her body type wasn't right, that she just didn't have what was required for a professional ballet dancer. And that there was nothing she could do about it. Ballet would never be anything more than a hobby for her.

The girl must have read this in her expression. "I'm not? I'm not going to be a dancer?"

"I didn't say that," Amy said quickly. "I don't know everything that's going to happen."

But apparently, the girl believed she did. Consternation crossed her face, and she ran out of the bathroom.

Amy stared after her helplessly. Tasha knew what Amy must be feeling and put a comforting arm around her.

"There's nothing you can do about it," she said. "It's not your fault."

Maybe not. But gazing into her best friend's sympathetic eyes, Amy had to wonder just how many more dreams she was going to crush with her so-called gift.

ten 10

Was this what a migraine felt like? Amy wondered. As if there were a million people screaming in your head?

She wasn't going to wait for Tasha at their usual spot on the school steps after the last bell. There was no way she could face the crowd who would be waiting and demanding to know their futures. Hordes of classmates, with hopes and fantasies of the future, just waiting for the great psychic Amy Candler to come out and stomp all over their dreams. Moving rapidly toward the back exit of the school after the last bell, she passed Chris at his locker and stopped.

"Could you give Tasha a message? She's waiting for me on the steps, and I—I have to do something. Just tell her to go home without me, okay?"

"Sure," Chris said, but Amy wondered whether Tasha would get the message. Chris had a lot of other stuff on his mind, and she saw it all. It was as clear to her as a DVD on a big-screen television.

The new homeless shelter, nastier than the one he'd been in before. The smell—it nauseated him. Fights broke out every five minutes. A gang of real bad guys rifled through everyone's stuff and stole anything worth taking. Too few workers tried to calm folks down. Drug addicts screamed all night long.

She didn't want to know this—any more than she wanted to see accidents about to happen or grandfathers who were going to die or kids who would never achieve their ambitions.

"Thanks" was all Amy said, and she hurried on. The halls were extremely noisy, like they always were after school, with kids yelling to each other and locker doors slamming. But the noises in her head were even louder. It seemed that every person she passed was thinking something she could hear.

I hope my father gets that new job. We could move to a bigger house, and I could have my own room. . . .

But that girl's father wasn't going to get the job, and she was going to be sharing a room with her whiny kid sister for two more long years.

Mom's going out with that nice man again tonight. He's so cool, I hope they get married. . . .

But they wouldn't.

The orthodontist appointment is at four; maybe he'll say it's time to take my braces off. . . .

It wasn't going to happen.

At least her math teacher was cheerful. He was actually smiling as he came toward her, talking with the nice new cafeteria lady. They parted, and as Mr. Henderson strode past Amy, she could hear him thinking.

Fantastic! They aced the quiz again. Standardized test scores are going to soar. I'll be teacher of the year; I'll get the twenty-thousand-dollar award. . . .

So that was why he wanted to be teacher of the year. He didn't care about students or how well they did. How depressing.

. . . Don't care how they feel, they're worthless kids; none of them are going to amount to anything, no great loss . . .

Amy's head began to throb. Henderson's thoughts were more than just depressing. How did the other teachers feel about the students? Did they all despise the kids the way he did?

She didn't want to know. But she would know. The voices would keep coming, the visions would appear. Unless, unless . . .

The bus left her off right in front of the hospital. She hurried around to the emergency room entrance and went inside.

The waiting room was packed with sick and injured people and others who were waiting for those who were being treated. Amy went to the nurses' station.

"I need to see Dr. David Hopkins," she said. "It's an emergency."

The nurse looked at her doubtfully, and Amy couldn't blame her. She didn't look sick or injured. "What's your problem?" the nurse asked.

"It's personal," Amy said. "Could you tell him Amy Candler is here?"

The nurse still looked doubtful, but she motioned for Amy to have a seat in the waiting room while she went in search of Dr. Dave.

It was pure torture, sitting there, surrounded by unhappy people. The thoughts came hard and fast. People in pain, people who were frightened, a woman thinking her husband would die, a man waiting for a doctor's diagnosis of his son . . . Was there anyone thinking happy thoughts? She probed the room, seeking a person who wasn't miserable.

She finally found a man who'd come into the emergency room to have some stitches removed. He was hoping he might have a little scar, because he thought it would make him look mysterious and romantic. And he was generally pleased with himself because he had quit smoking two weeks earlier. He was using a nicotine patch, so he hadn't had serious withdrawal symptoms. Interesting, how those patches worked. The nicotine was absorbed through the skin into the bloodstream. . . .

But then the man's name was called, and Amy couldn't learn anything more about nicotine patches. Frantically, her mind searched for other interesting— not depressing—thoughts. The nurse over there was happy because she'd just assisted in a successful surgical procedure. That doctor walking briskly past the waiting room area . . . she was excited about some new research on a chemical solution that would indicate the presence of toxic elements in foods. . . .

"Amy Candler?"

Amy jumped up and followed the nurse. Down a hall, in a small examination room, Dr. Dave was waiting for her.

"Would you like me to stay, Dr. Hopkins?" the nurse asked.

"Thank you, Ms. Jones, but that won't be necessary."

Dr. Dave never let any of the other medical staff hang around when he was examining Amy, or even when he was just talking to her. They couldn't risk revealing the truth of her unique genetic makeup.

Amy didn't even wait for Dr. Hopkins to ask her what was wrong. The second the nurse closed the door, she started talking.

"I think it was the lightning. It did something to my head. And I thought it was cool, but now I don't like it, and I can't stop it, and—"

"Whoa, slow down," Dr. Dave said. "Start from the beginning."

Amy took a deep breath and told him the whole story—how she suddenly knew what people were thinking and what was going to happen. As she spoke, she could hear how crazy it all sounded. But Dr. Dave listened carefully and didn't once accuse her of fabricating or exaggerating the story.

When she had finished her tale, Dr. Dave wanted to run a few tests on her brain. They were basically the same tests he'd run just after the accident—X rays, scans, brain waves, blood. But an hour later, with the results in front of him, he didn't have an answer.

"You don't have a normal brain," he told her. "But that's not news, is it? I'm going to have to study these results and do some research before I can figure out what happened."

"But what am I going to do in the meantime?" Amy wailed. "I can't stand knowing all this awful stuff!"

Dr. Dave considered her plight. "I have a suggestion," he said finally. "Now, this is just a theory, and it may not work, but I think it's worth a try. This new talent of yours—"

"You mean, this curse," Amy muttered.

"Whatever you want to call it. But if it is a talent, or a skill, it would have to be practiced. Like dancing, or singing—if you don't practice, the talent fades. Or if it's a physical condition, like a muscle, not using it could make it disappear altogether."

"So you're saying if I consciously try not to read minds or see futures, I could lose the ability?"

"Precisely," the doctor said. "It's a possibility."

There was a rap on the door, and before Dr. Dave could respond, the door opened. "Oh! I'm sorry, I didn't know you were with anyone."

"That's all right, Claire. What do you need?"

Amy recognized the white-coated woman. She was the doctor from the waiting room who had been so excited about a new medicine or something. She was still excited.

"I want to leave this with you," she said, placing a small vial on Dr. Dave's desk. "It's that serum I've been testing."

Dr. Dave knew what she was referring to. "The solution that detects drugs?" he asked.

She nodded. "It reacts to common poisons, also chemical compounds used in making speed and other drugs that affect brain behavior. I'll show you." From her pocket, she took a piece of bread. "I merely touched this bread with an infinitesimal dab of a narcotic drug. Now, watch what happens when I drop some solution on it."

She opened the vial, and with tiny eyedropper she extracted a bit of the colorless fluid. Then she emptied the dropper onto the bread. Immediately, the fluid turned bright green and began to bubble.

"Interesting," Dr. Hopkins said. "Can I hold on to this? I'd like to run some tests."

"Of course," the other doctor said. "I've got a liter of it back in my lab." She turned to leave, but at that moment something occurred to Amy.

"Excuse me," she said, "but you should be very careful with poisons and chemicals. And make sure you wear thick gloves."

The doctor was puzzled. "Why?"

"The chemicals could hurt the baby, couldn't they? I

mean, if they get into your bloodstream." The doctor stared at her. "You're pregnant, aren't you?" Amy asked.

The doctor's eyes widened. "I'm *trying* to become pregnant. I haven't been tested yet. What makes you think I'm pregnant?"

Amy avoided Dr. Dave's eyes. She was doing exactly what he'd told her *not* to do. She stammered what she hoped would be a believable response.

"Well, you—you have this glow, in your cheeks. Very maternal."

The woman eyed her strangely, but then she smiled. "Who knows? Excuse me, I think I'll run down to the pharmacy and pick up a pregnancy test." She left the office with the smile still on her face.

"Amy," Dr. Dave said reprovingly.

"Okay, okay, I'll try harder," Amy said.

"And come back on Monday after school," he ordered her. "I'd like to run these tests again."

"Okay," Amy said. But she hoped that maybe by Monday she wouldn't need them.

eleven

"Well, you're certainly looking more cheerful today," Nancy Candler commented at breakfast Monday morning.

"Yeah, I'm in a pretty good mood," Amy told her.

"Any special reason?"

Amy hesitated. "Oh, not really. It's a nice day out. The sun's shining."

"This is southern California, Amy," her mother reminded her. "The sun is almost always shining."

Amy just smiled. Maybe someday she'd tell Nancy about her brief career as a fortune-teller. But not just now. Not until she was absolutely sure she'd kicked the habit.

It hadn't been easy over the weekend, especially when she went to the mall with her mother on Saturday. All those people, all those potential minds to read and futures to see. But every time she was tempted, she fought back the urge and stopped herself from getting any more than a glimpse. Sunday evening they went to a movie, and she almost had a relapse. A man sitting just in front of her had been worried that he'd left an iron plugged in at home and that it would start a fire. She wanted to reassure him that nothing would happen, and it took a lot of effort to stop hearing and seeing. But that was the only really bad moment.

Tasha arrived on time to go to school, but *she* certainly didn't look cheerful.

"How was your date with Peter?" Amy asked. "I tried to call you yesterday but you weren't home."

"We went to see my grandmother." Tasha sighed. "The date was okay, I guess. Peter came back here with me afterward, and he kept asking when Eric would be home. I swear, I got the feeling that he was more interested in Eric than me! Isn't that ridiculous?" She peered at Amy closely. "Isn't it? Do you think you could check into his head and find out for me?"

"I can't," Amy said. "I don't do that anymore." She told Tasha about Dr. Dave's advice.

Tasha understood. "It's too bad you couldn't just know the good things that are going to happen to people."

"I know," Amy agreed. "But it doesn't work that way. So I'm just not reading minds or looking into futures at all anymore."

It wasn't that easy, though. Amy raced past the kids who were waiting on the steps, but that wasn't her only problem. Reminders of her gift—or curse or whatever it was—kept coming back to her. When she walked into school, she saw some kids with a gigantic get-well card, asking people to sign it.

"It's for Michelle Unser," one girl explained. "She broke her leg skiing this weekend." Just as Amy had known she would. She hated to ask the next question, but she had to. "Do you know a friend of hers?" Amy described the girl who had wanted to know if her grandfather would recover.

"Yeah, that's Hilary Woods."

"She's not here today," another girl said. "Her grandfather died."

Amy began getting visions of *this* girl with a bad case of the flu, but she blocked the images quickly. She signed the card and went on to her homeroom.

Linda Riviera was the first one to hit her up for a peek into the future. "Am I going to get my own TV for my birthday next week?" she asked.

"I haven't got the slightest idea," Amy replied.

Linda turned to the girl on her other side. "See, I *told* you it was just a big act."

It was bad, having Linda mock her like this, but Amy resisted the urge to prove her wrong. She gave herself a mental pat on the back for doing the right thing.

It wasn't long before she had the opportunity to pat herself again. A couple of boys cornered her in the hall between classes. They were both very cool ninth graders, and Amy had to admit to feeling a little thrilled that they actually knew her name.

She wasn't thrilled with their request, though. "We heard you could see into the future," one of them said. "We've got this great idea."

The other one explained it. "You could come up with next week's lottery number! It's worth fifty million dollars, and we could split it three ways."

They both looked so hopeful, she hated to disappoint them, but she had to. "I'm sorry," she said. "I can't do that. I don't have the gift anymore."

"You're kidding!" they cried out in unison.

"No," she said regretfully. "I guess it just sort of faded away."

From their expressions, she knew she was being a dreamcrusher again, but at least this time it didn't feel so terrible.

By lunchtime, the word had gotten around that Amy Candler had lost her gift, so people weren't bugging her for information. Peter, though, hadn't heard the news. He was talking to Tasha in the cafeteria when Amy approached with her tray, and he hit her with a question before she could even sit down.

"We're not having another pop quiz in math today, are we?"

Tasha helped her out. "Amy doesn't know. She can't see into the future anymore."

"Oh. Too bad." Peter turned back to Tasha. "So, maybe I'll come by your house this afternoon."

"Yeah, whatever," Tasha replied listlessly. Peter didn't seem to notice her unenthusiastic tone.

"You don't like him now, do you?" Amy was sympathetic but secretly relieved. Her relief was short-lived.

"I still like him," Tasha said sadly. "But I can't help feeling he doesn't really care about me. He just wants to shoot baskets with Eric. I'm really depressed." She picked up the glazed doughnut from her plate and brought it toward her mouth.

Amy snatched it away. "You'll just feel worse if you break your diet," she told Tasha.

"Yeah, I guess you're right."

Amy put the doughnut, along with her own, in her backpack to give to Chris in math. But just as she was on her way to that class, she heard his name over the loudspeaker.

"Chris Skinner, please report immediately to the principal's office."

Amy was alarmed. People weren't summoned to see Dr. Noble unless something really serious was going on. "I have to find out what's happening," she told Tasha. "I'll see you in class."

She hurried to the administrative wing and found a very unhappy-looking Chris sitting in the waiting area just outside the principal's office.

"What's wrong?" she asked him.

"There was an investigation at the shelter this morning," he told her. "I got out as fast as I could, but a cop spotted me. I guess he got my name from someone there, and he traced me here." He cocked his head toward the door. "He's in there now, talking to Dr. Noble."

The principal's door opened, and a uniformed police officer came out. Dr. Noble looked very serious, but she spoke to Chris kindly. "Chris, you can come in now."

Looking like he was facing the execution chamber,

Chris slithered off of his chair and went inside. Amy stared after him in dismay. She had no idea what would happen to him now.

Then she noticed that the police officer was looking at her. She realized he looked familiar.

"You're Amy Candler, aren't you?" he asked. "Jan's friend?"

That's where she'd seen him before, at Jan's birthday party. He was Mr. Rosen, Jan's father. "Yes, I'm Amy."

"Jan told me about your psychic abilities," he said. "I wanted to ask you if you could help us out with something." By *us* he meant the police, and before Amy could tell him that she was no longer a psychic, he told her what he wanted.

"We've had an anonymous note at headquarters. It might mean nothing—we get prank notes and phone calls all the time. But this one said there's a teacher here at Parkside who's trying to hurt students. Something about feeding them drugs to make their brains work harder. I was thinking, if you could use your abilities—"

Amy didn't let him go any farther. "Excuse me," she interrupted. "But I can't. You see, I don't have the psychic talent anymore."

"Oh." Officer Rosen frowned. "Well, if you get the talent back—"

"I won't," Amy told him. She felt awful, telling him she wouldn't help uncover a criminal. "But if I hear anything, I'll let you know."

"Fine, fine," he murmured, and left the office. He was clearly disappointed. But she had to get back to being an ordinary nonpsychic kid. She couldn't help him.

twelve

A teacher poisoning kids with drugs. How horrible. Amy just hoped the anonymous note had been written by a prankster. What kind of teacher would do something like that?

It was hard pushing that thought out of her mind while she sat in math class. Maybe because Mr. Henderson was the kind of teacher who *would* do something like that.

Amy gazed at him thoughtfully as he demonstrated an equation on the blackboard. He'd certainly wanted the kids to get smarter so the scores would improve and he could be teacher of the year. But would he go this far to get what he wanted? No, it was a crazy idea. Besides, it wasn't like he ever gave the students anything to eat or drink. If he was passing out drugs, she'd know about it.

She had something else to worry about too. Chris. He hadn't shown up for class. What could be going on in Dr. Noble's office? What would happen to him?

And Tasha . . . poor Tasha. How was she going to feel when she found out her suspicions of Peter were true? Amy knew she'd better be ready to provide a shoulder for crying on.

There was one benefit to having all these worries on her mind. It was easier to block out her classmates' thoughts. But it was also easier to space out. Which was why she walked out of class at the bell without doing something extremely vital and important.

"Hey! You!" Mr. Henderson hadn't yet learned the names of all his new students.

"Yes?" Amy asked.

"Where's my pencil? You didn't leave your pencil on my desk! Give it to me!"

Amy fumbled in her backpack and took out the stolen property. "I'm sorry, I wasn't thinking," she apologized.

"You kids never do," he grumbled, snatching the pencil from her hand.

The guy was awfully possessive about his stupid, ordinary yellow pencils, Amy thought. He was definitely one of the weirder teachers around.

After school, Amy caught the bus for her appointment with Dr. Dave. She was looking forward to telling him that his advice was working, so that maybe she wouldn't have to go through all those brain tests again.

Once again, the hospital waiting room was filled with unhappy people. But this time Amy didn't hang around. She went directly to Dr. Dave's office. The door was ajar, but he wasn't there. She figured he'd just gone to the rest room. She went inside to wait.

Amy looked for a magazine to read but was disappointed not to find one. She wasn't comfortable just sitting around. Something was bothering her, but she couldn't put her finger on what it was. Something in the back of her mind refused to come to the surface. She'd been trying so hard *not* to think too much, and she was afraid of concentrating on anything, even her own thoughts.

But this thought she couldn't identify was nagging her. When had it started bothering her? When she had come into the waiting room? What had she been thinking about? Chris, Tasha, the tests that Dr. Dave might run? The man who had quit smoking with the help of a nicotine patch—

The man with the nicotine patch! The nicotine in the patch was absorbed into the bloodstream through the skin. She gasped. Could other substances be absorbed through the skin by another means? Something you held—like a pencil?

A small vial on Dr. Dave's desk caught her eye. The solution that revealed the presence of poisons and drugs. Slowly, Amy rose and went toward the desk. She picked up the vial and examined it.

A sound made her whirl around. The doctor who was conducting the research on the solution stood in the doorway. "Oh, hi!" the woman said. "You were here last Friday, weren't you?"

"Yes," Amy said. Behind her back, her fingers closed around the vial. "I have another appointment with Dr. Hopkins."

"He just went out to consult on an emergency," she said. "I came by to pick up something." She went to his desk. "Hmm . . . I wonder where he put it. It was a small vial . . ."

Amy looked at her innocently.

"Well, I don't want to poke around in his drawers. I'll come back later." The doctor smiled at Amy. "By the way, you were right! I *am* pregnant! Could you really see a special glow on my face?"

Amy gulped. "Yes, absolutely—a beautiful rosy maternal glow. Listen, could you tell Dr. Hopkins I couldn't wait? Thanks!"

And with the vial hidden in her fist, she fled.

thirteen 13

"I'll bet it's Henderson," Tasha said at lunch the next day, handing her glazed doughnut over to Amy. She was so intrigued by Amy's theory and plan that she wasn't even tempted. "It *has* to be Henderson. I can't think of any other teacher as mean as he is. He hates students. He doesn't care about us at all. Even *I* know that, and I can't read his mind. And that would explain why he makes us use *his* pencils."

"And why he keeps them locked up in his drawer," Amy added. "That way he can control the dosage."

"When are you going to test the pencils?" Tasha asked.

"As soon as he hands them out in class," Amy told her. "I'll do it under the desk, where he can't see. And when the green bubbles form, I'll ask for a rest-room pass, and then I'll call Jan's father from the pay phone down by the gym."

Tasha shook her head sadly. "I thought Henderson was just weird. Now I know he's truly evil. He'd feed us drugs just to be teacher of the year."

"And win twenty thousand dollars," Amy reminded her. She wrapped the glazed doughnuts in a napkin and tossed them in her backpack. "Have you seen Chris today?"

"I saw him in the hall last period."

Amy was relieved. If he was here at school, nothing too terrible could have happened to him. He wasn't in a juvenile reformatory or anything like that. "I've been dying to tell him about Henderson." She looked around the cafeteria. "There's Peter. You think I should tell him? I'll bet he'd love to hear about this, he hates Henderson so much."

Tasha's face darkened, and she shook her head. "Peter's a jerk. I'm absolutely positive now. He came over after school yesterday to shoot baskets with Eric, and he barely said hello to me. That's the only reason he asked me out—to meet my brother, the basketball star."

"I know," Amy said, and then wished she could take back the words. It was too late.

Tasha's mouth fell open. "You knew? You read it in his mind?'

Amy nodded.

"Why didn't you tell me?"

"I couldn't," Amy said. "I didn't want to give you bad news. All last week I was crushing people's dreams, and I felt really crummy about it."

Tasha was completely unsympathetic. "So you let me go ahead and make a fool of myself over Peter, when you knew all along that he was just using me to get to Eric. And you call yourself a best friend!"

"I'm sorry," Amy said, "but—"

Tasha gave her no opportunity to justify what she'd done, or hadn't done. She rose from the table, snatched up her tray, and walked off.

Amy was shocked. She knew Tasha would be mad, but not *this* mad. "Tasha, wait!" she called, but Tasha was on the other side of the cafeteria, dropping her tray on the conveyor belt. Then she marched out the door.

Amy hurried to the belt and dumped her own tray. Maybe if she headed toward math class she could pull Tasha aside before the bell rang and try again to apologize.

But Chris was waiting for her outside the classroom, and he looked like he wasn't very happy with her either.

"I brought you doughnuts," she started to say, but he wasn't interested.

"You must have seen that coming," he said. "The investigation at the new shelter. Why didn't you warn me?"

"I've been trying not to use the power," Amy explained. "I want to lose it, and Dr. Dave said it might wear off if I tried not to see futures or read minds."

"Well, you could have made an exception for me," Chris replied. "I'm in a real fix now. They've got me staying at Children's Services, and in two days I'm being sent to a foster home!"

"Where?" Amy asked in dismay.

"Around here somewhere. I'm supposed to be staying here at Parkside."

"Well, that's a relief," Amy said, but clearly Chris didn't share her feeling.

"Some relief. What if this family treats me like dirt? Or even worse, what if they try to act like parents?"

Amy didn't know what to say, and fortunately she didn't have to say anything. The bell rang, and they had to go to their seats. Mr. Henderson ordered them to be quiet, and then he handed out pencils. As soon as she received hers, Amy fumbled in her backpack and pulled out the vial.

She tried to catch Tasha's eye, but Tasha wouldn't even look at her. She was really mad. Amy wasn't quite sure how she was going to make this up to her. It would take some serious thinking—but not now. She had an experiment to perform.

Thank goodness the class was large. Mr. Henderson was still passing out pencils. Concealing her hands under the desk, Amy carefully unscrewed the vial and let a drop fall on her pencil.

Nothing happened. She waited and watched, but no green bubbles began to form.

Frowning, she wondered if maybe the chemical solution hadn't touched the part of the pencil that was treated with the drug. She added a couple more drops, letting them run down the sides of the pencil until it was completely coated. Still nothing. All she had was a wet pencil.

"Young lady, pay attention!"

Amy looked up. "Yes sir," she murmured. Again, she tried to catch Tasha's eye to show her the pencil, but again, Tasha's gaze was fixed on the front of the room.

There was no pop quiz that day. Students were called up to solve equations Henderson had written on the board. She wondered if maybe she should test the chalk with the solution, but she didn't really hope to learn anything from that. No one held the chalk all that long.

When class was over, Amy saw Tasha leave the room in a hurry, and she knew her best friend wouldn't be waiting for her outside. But Chris was.

"Listen," he said, "I'll give you a chance to make it up to me."

"Okay," Amy said. "What can I do?"

"Tell me what the foster family is going to be like."

"What?"

"So I can be prepared. Look into my future and tell me what to expect."

"Chris!" Amy exclaimed. "I just told you, I'm not supposed to do this anymore. Not if I want it to go away."

Chris's face darkened. His mouth was set in a tight grimace—and when he finally spoke, he barely moved his lips.

"Thanks a lot, Amy," he said sarcastically, and walked away.

Amy stared after him as he disappeared into the crowd. And then she had a special ache, one that she could identify immediately. She was about to burst into tears.

She made it into a rest room. The bell rang, but she

ignored it. At least the rest room was empty now, and she could cry as loudly as she wanted to.

What else could go wrong in her life? Her best friend and her almost-boyfriend were furious with her. Half the kids at school were annoyed that she'd stopped telling fortunes. Her pencil theory was all wrong, and now she had no idea who might be responsible for drugging the students.

She reached for a piece of toilet paper to blow her nose, but naturally, the roll was empty. Sniffling, she rummaged around in her backpack for a tissue. Her finger touched something wet and sticky.

She pulled it out. It was one of the doughnuts she'd tossed in the pack at lunch. She must have replaced the vial without screwing the top back on tightly, because the solution had spilled onto the doughnut.

Which was now covered in green bubbles.

fourteen

Amy didn't spend much time observing the green foam. And she didn't need to keep searching for a tissue—the tears had dried up on their own. Clutching the doughnut and her backpack, she ran out of the rest room, down the stairs, and straight to the cafeteria.

Lunch period was over, and the cafeteria was deserted. Chairs were upturned on the tables, and the floor had already been mopped, but she figured there might still be people in the kitchen cleaning up. She started in that direction, but before she reached the doors leading into the kitchen, a woman came out.

It was the doughnut woman, Ms. Robertson. She saw

the green doughnut in Amy's hand and gasped. "Good heavens! What happened?"

"There's something in these doughnuts," Amy told her. "Something bad, like poison, or a speed drug. Do you know how it could have gotten there?"

Ms. Robertson was taken aback, and she looked offended. "My dear, I only use the best ingredients in these doughnuts. There aren't even any preservatives in them. They're freshly made every morning."

"Then someone's been adding the drugs after you finish making them," Amy told her. "Who can get their hands on them?"

"Well, anyone who works in the cafeteria, of course. It's not like the food is kept under lock and key. People are in and out of the kitchen all morning."

"What about Mr. Henderson?"

The woman stared at her. "Who?"

"The math teacher. Does he ever come into the kitchen?"

Ms. Robertson shook her head. "No. Now, if you'll excuse me, I have to get home." She turned and hurried out of the cafeteria. That was when Amy got a little whiff of something in the woman's head. It wasn't clear at all. Concern, maybe. Or confusion. Or something darker.

It bothered her. Amy had a feeling that maybe Ms. Robertson knew something she wasn't telling.

Making an instant decision, Amy reached out to read the woman's mind. It was the only way to learn for sure what was going on. So she concentrated—but nothing happened. She tried again, listening hard, but there was nothing to hear. And then Ms. Robertson was gone.

So Dr. Dave had been right. Not using the gift had made it fade away. Old-fashioned thinking would be necessary.

Amy took a chair off a table and sat down to think.

It didn't make sense. Mr. Henderson didn't have access to the doughnuts. And no one who worked in the cafeteria had any reason to drug students. Maybe if that awful lady had been still working here, she would have done something like that just out of meanness. Henderson was the only person who had a real motive. Maybe he hid the stuff in the cafeteria, and that was how it got into the doughnuts.

Amy went through the doors that Ms. Robertson had used, her super-senses alert. She heard something. It was very soft—barely more than a whisper of a sound. Sort of like breathing, but not exactly. A mouse?

Moving cautiously, Amy headed in the direction of a

large storage unit where metal canisters of sugar and salt and other ingredients were kept. Behind the unit she located the source of the noise.

A balding man, wearing a white jacket and a name tag—MR. MOORE, CAFETERIA MANAGER—was sitting in his usual wheelchair. A rope held his wrists together, and a dishrag was stuffed in his mouth.

"Mr. Moore! What happened?" Amy rushed forward and uncovered his mouth. "Who did this to you?"

"Robertson!" he told her. He took a deep breath. "I was asking her some questions, and she got nervous. She tied me up and ran off."

"But why?" Amy asked as she untied the rope that bound his hands. "What kind of questions were you asking her?"

He hesitated, as if reluctant to confide in a student. Then he relented. "I have this—this talent, I guess you could call it. An understanding of people. Like an instinct. I know when they're up to no good."

Amy's eyes widened. "You can read minds?"

Mr. Moore looked at her like she was nuts. "No, dear. It comes from the way they act, their expressions, their mannerisms. Or what they say. Do you remember that woman who used to work in here? The one who never smiled?"

Amy nodded.

"I saw the way she looked at students," he continued. "The way her eyes narrowed, and her mouth went down. I could tell she didn't like the kids. And I don't want people like that working in my cafeteria."

Amy guessed what had happened. "So you told Dr. Noble, and the woman was fired."

Mr. Moore nodded.

"But Ms. Robertson seemed so nice!" Amy said. "What made you think she was up to no good?"

"It was something to do with those doughnuts," he told her. "I suggested that we stop serving them daily. Too much sugar, you know. Bad for the teeth. But she was so insistent! It bothered me." Then he looked a little embarrassed. "I started to get some crazy ideas. There used to be a teen club here in town, where the owner was slipping drugs into the kids' sodas or something. He was part of a drug distribution ring, trying to get kids addicted without their knowledge. Then the kids would have to start buying drugs on their own."

Amy knew what he was talking about. She remembered the club very well, and the owner, who was now in prison.

"So Ms. Robertson was part of a drug ring?" she mused.

Now Mr. Moore looked even more embarrassed. "Well, actually, I have no proof of that. That's why I didn't tell Dr. Noble my suspicions. I just sent an anonymous note to the police asking them to investigate whether someone at Parkside Middle School was pushing drugs to students."

It was beginning to make sense. "And the cops assumed you meant a teacher," she murmured. She felt a sudden chill, as if someone was coming up behind her. She whirled around.

"Yes, people think only teachers have brains," Ms. Robertson declared. "No one would suspect a cafeteria worker. Well, this cafeteria worker is smarter than you think. And stronger too."

With that, she leaped forward and grabbed Amy around the neck. Mr. Moore immediately tried to ram her with his wheelchair, but she kicked it—and him— over. Then she focused all her energies on Amy.

She *was* strong. Fortunately, Amy was stronger. With a little effort, Amy got the woman's hands off her neck and pushed her to the ground. The woman got back up, but Amy grabbed her wrists and held tight.

The door to the kitchen opened.

"What's going on here?" Dr. Noble cried in horror.

"This student went crazy!" Ms. Robertson shrieked. "She came in here and attacked Mr. Moore. When I tried to help, she hit me!"

From his position on the floor, Mr. Moore yelled, "That's not true—she's lying!"

Dr. Noble was clearly confused. "Amy, let Ms. Robertson go! Immediately!"

Instinctively, Amy obeyed the principal—and the woman fled from the kitchen.

"Dr. Noble, she's a criminal! She's trying to drug students!" Amy told her as they pulled Mr. Moore's wheelchair upright.

"That's correct," Mr. Moore said.

Dr. Noble groaned. "Oh no, don't tell me there have been *two* pushers at Parkside."

Amy stared at her. "What do you mean, two?"

"The police are here right now," Dr. Noble told her sadly. "Arresting Mr. Henderson."

"They've got the wrong person!" Amy yelled. As she ran out, she could hear Dr. Noble talking to Mr. Moore.

"You really must cut down on the amount of sugar the students are getting. It's making them hyper."

Amy flew down the hall, up the stairs, and out of the building. In the parking lot, she saw a police car with a flashing light. Jan's father and another policeman were putting Mr. Henderson into the back of the car.

"Wait!" she called. "Wait! I have information!" She

caught up to the officers. "Why are you arresting this man?"

"We've been trailing him for days," Officer Rosen told her. "And we put a tap on his phone. He's been buying drugs and feeding them to students to make them study harder."

"Because he wants to become teacher of the year," the other policeman added.

"But what we still don't know is how he got the drugs to the kids," Officer Rosen went on. "We don't have any evidence. We know the kids are getting drugged, but we don't know how."

Suddenly Amy remembered seeing Henderson talking to the cafeteria lady. It was just when all the voices in her head had been overwhelming her. She'd been too distracted to notice. Now she didn't need to read Mr. Henderson's mind—all she had to do was use pure logic.

"He had a partner," she told the police. "Ms. Robertson, who worked in the cafeteria. She got the drugs into the students." She reached into her backpack and pulled out the remnants of the doughnut.

"Here's your evidence."

fifteen

What a day. When the final bell rang, all Amy wanted to do was go home, turn on the TV, and play couch potato while devouring an entire box of cookies. She wanted no more confrontations. Which was why she wasn't thrilled to see Chris waiting by her locker. She'd already spent enough time defending herself that day.

But Chris didn't go on the attack again. "I'm sorry," he said. "I shouldn't have asked you to predict the future for me. It wasn't your responsibility to tell me what's going to happen." His eyes were pleading. "You can tell that I really mean this, can't you?"

Amy nodded. "But that's not because I'm reading your mind. I can't do it anymore anyway," Amy replied. She told him how she'd tried to read Ms. Robertson's mind and failed. Chris actually seemed relieved.

"So you're normal again," he said.

Amy smiled and shrugged. Of course, she would never be normal, but Chris didn't know that. Not yet. Maybe someday, if all went well . . .

They walked toward the exit together. On the way, they passed Dr. Noble talking to a teacher. "We'll start looking for a replacement immediately," the principal was saying. "But in the meantime, you'll have to take Henderson's classes."

"That teacher's furious," Amy said.

Chris was puzzled. "I thought you said you couldn't hear thoughts anymore."

Amy laughed. "Chris, the teacher's just been told that her class size has tripled. You don't have to be a mind reader to figure out how she feels!"

Nor did Amy have to be a mind reader to know that Tasha was still angry with her. She wasn't waiting for Amy to walk home from school together.

At home, Amy put her plan into motion. She opened a box of cookies and poured herself a large glass of milk. Snuggling on the couch with the remote control, she tried to watch TV and relax.

For once, however, this comforting routine didn't work. Probably because she was still feeling so bad about Tasha. Or maybe it was the *thump, thump, thump* of the basketball on the carport next door.

She gave up on the TV and went outside. As she suspected, Eric was shooting hoops. And Tasha was outside too, sitting on her steps and looking glum. She glanced up as Amy approached, and she looked like she was about to speak, but the hurt was still in her eyes and she looked away.

Eric was willing to talk to her, though, and for the first time in a long time, he actually seemed eager to.

"Hey, I heard you've got ESP!"

Amy glanced at Tasha, who wouldn't meet her eyes, before turning back to Eric. "What about it?"

"Can you see into the future and all that?" he asked.

"Why? Is there something you want to know?"

"Sure!" He scratched his head. "Um . . . is my basketball team going to the state finals this year?"

Amy pretended to concentrate. She put both her hands to her temples, closed her eyes, and made a humming noise. "I'm beginning to see something . . . yes, I'm definitely getting a vision."

"What?" Eric asked excitedly. "Do you see my team?"

"Yes . . . yes! I see the team at the state finals . . . I see the team *winning* the state finals."

"No kidding!" Eric exclaimed.

"Wait a minute," Amy said. "There's a condition! Something has to happen for the team to win."

"What's the condition? More practice?"

"No." Amy squeezed her eyes shut. What was Tasha's least favorite household chore? She remembered.

"Vacuuming."

"Huh?"

"If the guys on the basketball team start vacuuming their homes on a regular basis, the team will win."

"You've got to be kidding."

Amy opened her eyes. "Nope. That's what I see."

"What do vacuum cleaners have to do with basketball?" Eric demanded.

Amy shrugged. "NAC."

"Huh?"

"Not a clue."

"Oh." Eric frowned. "Sounds crazy to me."

Amy just shrugged again.

Eric bounced the ball a few more times. "I'm going to get something to eat," he announced, and went inside his house. Amy went to the steps and sat down next to Tasha.

"Tasha, I'm sorry I made you angry. I don't know if I should have told you what Peter was thinking or not. But you can't stay mad at me, you just can't. If you

132

weren't my best friend anymore, I don't know what I would do."

Tasha's eyes welled up. Just then, they both heard a sound coming from inside the house. A vacuum cleaner was running.

Tasha's eyes cleared and brightened. She looked at Amy. And as if on cue, they both started laughing. Then Tasha threw her arms around her.

"Amy Candler, you are undoubtedly the most fantastic very best friend anyone in the world could ever have!"

Don't miss

replica

#20

Like Father, Like Son

Chris Skinner, Amy's new boyfriend, comes from a broken home. He hasn't seen his father in, like, forever. And when his dad finally appears, it isn't to make up for Chris's miserable childhood. Mr. Skinner is ill—so ill that he needs a bone marrow transplant. Chris could be the perfect match. There's nothing strange in that, except—

What if ailing grown-ups could tap into a guaranteed reserve of healthy body parts?

What if innocent kids were being harmed?

What if *you* were bred to become an unwilling donor?

Amy knows she's blessed with superhuman genes, but no way, nohow is she going to let herself, or any other kid, fall prey to freakish sci-fi experiments!